CAR HEROIN TRAIN

Virginia Austin

Front and Back Cover designed by Billy Duffy
& Alisha Moore @Damonza.com
Lyric clipped in Chpt. 10: Johnny Thunders, "You Can't Put Your Arms
Around a Memory." Lyrics clipped in Chapter 11: LCD Soundsystem, "All
My Friends." Title of Chapter 11: ("I'm a Slave to Always Fucking Up")
blatantly stolen from lyric off of Beach Slang's "Filthy Luck."

Visit www.virginiaaustin.com

Printed in the United States of America

First Printing: October 2019
Melting Salvation Press, LLC

ISBN-13 978-0-9794085-4-0

For
Jeff Komada, Travis Hugo,
and Frank Trikur

My Dear Keira,

I am writing this to you as I anticipate a day when temptation will arrive at your doorstep and I will not be there to greet it with you. I, of course, cannot be everywhere. So, I am giving you these words of admonition as a stand-in for my absence. These claws of addiction are long and go in deep. They are unforgiving and they can be murderous. They kill not only the ones they are tearing into, but all of those near to the nest. Remember, my love, one death and the living all fall.

Death needs time for what it kills to grow in
—WILLIAM S. BURROUGHS

CONTENTS

SAVE ADDICTS – WIN VALUABLE PRIZES

AMANDA WAS SITTING ON THE COUCH, leaning over the coffee table with her head slumped forward. The palm of one hand she had pressed to her brow and was moving it around like a planchette on a spirit board. She had just drawn up half of what she had cooked on a kitchen spoon. She had just shot exactly the same amount into one of her good veins. There was victory in that. Half was what she had committed to on her new heroin diet. Half was just enough to get her high, and half was just enough to make her believe that she wasn't such a fucking loser like the rest of the users there.

A pause from the turntable and then another song began. The music wasn't what she would have played. None of the people there the ones she would have invited. On her face arrived an unconscious look of disdain, and from the coffee table, she picked the needle back up and aimed it across the room like a dart player. Everyone there she had in her sights. Suddenly though, the lights from the December Christmas tree that neither she nor her boyfriend had gotten around to taking down began to grow brighter. That power surge in her mind was however only an ephemeral spike and soon softened into a kaleidoscope of warm colors. She swayed a bit. And finally, the heroin pushed her over and she toppled onto the lap of the girl at the end of the couch. The girl rolled her eyes and stood up. Amanda grabbed the pillow and wrapped her arms around it like she was holding onto a piece of heaven. "Thank God," she said. "Thank God I'm not an addict like the rest of you here." It was the last whisper that came off her lips before her lids fell, and she left this world for one without the burden of gravity and all that other shit that makes you feel so goddamn heavy.

* * *

John stood with his ass balanced on the edge of the kitchen sink. He had the heel of one black boot kicking the bass beat against the cabinet door. He had his arms stretched out across the countertop and his fingers tapping to the toms. His head was bobbing to the song, but his eyes were locked on the only other person in the room. He was jonesing and he was pissed. The heroin had moved on out of his veins and the cocaine was on its last drip. It was just a little after ten in the evening, but his body needed more.

"Cut it the fuck out, will you," he shouted while swiping a wave of his atramentous-colored hair from off of his face.

"Cut what out?" his friend Jason asked from the folding table he was sitting at.

"That thing you're doing with your goddam jaw. It's annoying the shit out of me."

"I'm not doing anything with my jaw. And how could you even hear it anyway? All I hear is music. And now, you," Jason replied, and then placed the three of spades atop the red four of diamonds for his final move.

"I don't need to hear it. I can see it. Jesus, that twitch you got is messed up. You do it every time you're on blow."

"Witch? What witch?" Jason questioned as he gathered up the blue and white Bicycle playing cards and began to shuffle them.

"Oh, fuck me. Give me your phone. I'm gonna call that asshole myself."

"I just called him five minutes ago," Jason answered as he dealt himself out another game.

"Well, fucking ring him up again. This is bullshit. We've been waiting on this dickhead for over an hour now."

"He'll call. Don't worry. He's good about that shit."

"Yeah, he's good about it all right. The last time he was good about it was two fucking days later. Again, we're just two stupid motherfuckers looking to score. You know what we should be doing?"

"What?"

"What? That figures. You're a fucking idiot. What we should be doing is selling it our goddamn selves. Become entrepreneurs. Get a little start-up going just like that little prick Zuckerberg. Shit, everyone else in this city is dealing it. No fucking reason we can't get something going."

Jason guffawed as he set out an ace of hearts to the left of him.

"What's so fucking funny?"

"Nothing, man."

"No, say it. You found something I said funny, so let me in on it."

"It's junkie talk, man. That's why I laughed. You'd have all that shit in your veins before your first customer even came to the door."

John eased down from the countertop and walked over to him. As a queen was being placed onto a king, he lifted Jason by his armpits and dragged him over to the refrigerator. For a moment, he was losing himself in the cocaine eyes staring back at him. The dilated pupils were a millimeter from a full eclipse of his green irises. It was freaking him out, and after a shake of his head, he finally remembered what he was going to say.

"I'm no fucking junkie. I ain't living on no goddamn street with drool coming out of my mouth. You got that, motherfucker?"

"Yeah, I got it, asshole," Jason said, and then looked over John's shoulder as Amanda entered the kitchen.

Her gait was unsteady. Her face could barely be seen as the strands of blonde hair were covering most of it. She had on faded blue jeans, dirtied at one of the thighs by a smear of cigarette ash. She was barefoot, her toenails painted turquoise. She had on a white T-shirt with black printed words: "Save Addicts – Win Valuable Prizes." Around John's waist, she wrapped her arms and interlocked her fingers before her head fell hard against the top of his spine.

"There you are. I was looking for you," Amanda said with a slow delivery.

"Fuck, come on. Get off me, Amanda," John replied as he attempted to pry her hands away. She locked them tighter. "I said, get the fuck off of me. Jesus Christ. What is wrong with you?"

Frustrated, he grabbed her wrists and twisted. She barely felt a thing, but it did the trick. He spun around and Jason stepped away from the refrigerator. Amanda looked at John. She was about to put her hands on his chest when he gave her a shove that sent her over the chair and to the floor.

"Why in the hell do you make me do that shit? I told you to get the fuck off of me."

Jason walked over to Amanda and took a knee. He put a hand out to help her up. She reached to take it but withdrew when John came forward to put both of them in his shadow.

"Leave her there."

"I'm not leaving her on the floor. Come on, Amanda. Give me your hand."

"I said, leave her the fuck there."

"Fuck you," Jason replied, glancing up to John.

"Fuck me, huh? Okay," John said and walked over to the back door.

"Don't worry about him, Amanda. You're going to be okay. Just give me your hand."

"How about now?" John asked as he returned, an ash wood baseball bat in his hand. "You gonna leave her there or what?"

Jason shook his head and stood up. Before giving his reply, he stepped out of range of the Rawlings Adirondack.

"You're a fucking dick, you know that. It's just amazing she hasn't left your loser ass yet."

John lifted the bat and feigned a swat to the skull of his friend. Jason swung his head to the right but kept his body still as if he was okay with taking the hit.

"Now get the fuck out of here. I never want to see your face within a goddamn mile of this place. You are officially *persona non grata*."

"It'll only be temporary."

"And why the hell do you think that?"

"Because you'll be fucking dead soon, John. A needle in your arm and your eyes to the sky."

Jason took another look at Amanda. She seemed as if she was going to be okay. Her head had taken to rest on her right arm, and her eyes had closed for the night. He backed out of the room, and after crossing the threshold, threw up his middle finger to bid John farewell. John flipped the Adirondack, but it went no farther than the kitchen cabinet and bounced to the floor. He stepped over Amanda's body and went straight to the bedroom of their apartment.

KEROIN HILLS, USA

A S HE WALKED IN LINE WITH THE rest of the University of Chicago graduates and the bagpipes skirled "Scotland the Brave," Evan had only one thing on his mind. That was the quote by the American physicist Richard Feynman: "One does not, by knowing all the fundamental laws as we know them today, immediately obtain an understanding of anything much." Ironic as it seemed coming from a man who took a share of the Nobel Prize in Physics, Evan understood that in all likelihood it wasn't meant to have any tinge of irony whatsoever. He also understood the quote hinged on the word "immediately." For after all the knowledge is learned, there is still that lag in time when nothing at all is known. And so as he neared to within twenty feet of the stage, he decided that there was no better time in the eye of this unknowing than to leave now and find out why. Breaking rank, he stepped out of line and began heading back to where he had started the day. The girl from the

Guangdong province with whom he had been walking with gave him only a mere look from the corners of her eyes. She was moving forward. He, on the other hand, understood a step back was required before he could continue on.

"Evan Adamko," the presenting officer read from the list situated on the dais, just after he had called out the name Zhu Linyao.

From the crowd, a woman in her late forties stood up and took aim at the middle of the stage with her newly purchased camera. It was the absence of applause that prompted the presenting officer to look off to his right. A few polite seconds he waited before repeating the name, just a little louder than the first time and perhaps even a little sterner.

"Evan Adamko."

The woman from the crowd slowly lowered her camera to get a panoramic view of the stage. Perplexed, she searched about a few times before dropping back onto her folding chair. With a shrug of his shoulders, the presenting officer moved his finger down one name. He was also forging ahead.

* * *

On his way back to Rickert House, Evan Adamko took rest at the base of the Nuclear Energy bronze sculpture. While in previous visits he had taken time to stop and wonder over the creativity of man's destructive capacity, today it didn't even cross his mind. He took out his cell phone and began conducting a search for the next flight out of Chicago to the city of Buffalo. It didn't take long before the device was returned to his pocket. And it didn't take long before he was opening the door to the dorm in which he had sequestered himself for the last four years of his life.

He went straight to his closet. There he gave a toss of his graduation cap into the corner and there he stripped off his gown, which he balled up and unceremoniously shot into a corner. It was an uncharacteristic disposal for a young man who had exactly seven hangers of clothing, which were taxonomically sorted for each day of the week. Every Sunday night, after doing laundry, he matched seven pairs of pants with seven collared shirts. It saved time, he theorized. Time, which instead of waking up and deciding what to wear for the day, could be better spent.

Evan's roommate, Ashok, was sitting at a desk by the window with a laptop open. And though he had his headphones on and the volume raised loud, he was quite aware of the movement behind him. However, he was reluctant to step out of the Bollywood movie that once again was making him feel as if he was a young child in the New Delhi neighborhood of Karol Bagh. A moment later though the sound of something crashing to the floor was enough of a ripple in space to pull him back to reality. He paused his movie and spun around one hundred and eighty degrees.

"That is not good. Ganesh is for luck and prosperity, you know."

"Yes, I know, Ashok. You tell me every time you return home and bring me back another one," Evan said from a knee. He said while he was gathering up the pieces of the ceramic elephant that had come along for the ride as he was pulling his backpack down.

"The others cannot help the broken one."

"I didn't think they could," Evan said as he glanced up at the shelf to the other two elephants that were resting there. "But thank you for confirming my presupposition."

"You are welcome, my brother. That was a fast graduation. You are gone no longer than an hour."

"Yeah, they got through the ceremony pretty quick," Evan replied after he had finished moving the pile over to the inside of the closet. He was now stowing away the clothing he had decided to take with him when Ashok spoke again.

"I am sorry once again that I did not come, but I do not like endings. I do not even watch them in my Indian movies."

"That's okay, Ashok. Neither do I," Evan replied as he stood up and threw his backpack over his shoulder. "Okay, I'm out of here."

"Boy, my brother, when you are done with something, you are certainly done with it."

"I'm not leaving for good, Ashok. I just have to go somewhere. I'll be back in three or four days. I'll need my laptop, though."

"The best part is coming up. Deepika Padukone is about to do her dance number in *HNY*," Ashok answered, throwing a momentary look over his shoulder to the frozen screen.

"Ashok, you've already watched that scene about a thousand times."

"Yes, you are correct. And Deepika Padukone just keeps getting more and more beautiful every time I do."

"I'm serious. I need it. Can't you get your laptop back from what's her name?"

"Her name is Katrina. And she is in need of it."

"Why did you give it to her anyway?"

"Because I love her. That is why."

"You do understand there is zero probability of you ever hooking up with her."

"For that to be true, all possible outcomes would have to have zero probability."

"Yes," Evan said.

"I will get the laptop back from Katrina," Ashok said as he reached around and closed the cover.

"Thank you," Evan replied and walked over to Ashok, where his dearest friend handed him the laptop.

"Do you need the power cord?"

"It would help."

"Then that is in the top drawer of my desk. If I may ask, where are you going in such a hurry?"

"Down to the Florida Keys. I'll call you. Or e-mail you. Or something."

"What about your graduation party? This will not please your mother."

"What graduation party?"

"The graduation party your mother is giving to you tonight."

"Tonight? Why didn't anyone tell me about it?"

"Because the invitation said 'Do Not Tell Evan.' "

"God, why did she do that? She knows I didn't want a party."

"Because she loves you, my brother. That is why."

"Okay, she is probably walking over here right now. Just tell her . . . God, I don't know. Just tell her I left for Florida with my girlfriend to celebrate."

"Improbable."

"Why?"

"Because everyone knows that in your four years here, you have yet to feel the warm body of any one of the eligible girls from the student body."

"Whatever. Then just tell her I went to a conference on quantifying mathematical structure in complex models."

"That should work. Good luck on your journey, my brother."

"Thanks, Ashok."

After the door closed, Ashok pulled out a cell phone from his pocket. He scrolled through his movie roll, and within another minute or so, he was back at the Atlantis hotel with Deepika Padukone.

* * *

Evan raced down the stairs, taking out the steps two at a time. He figured his mother was probably wandering around campus, trying to navigate her way to his dorm room. It wasn't that he didn't want to see her. It was just that he didn't want to have to explain. And it wasn't as if she wouldn't have understood. It was because he didn't want to lie to her. He had misjudged, though. Not long after leaving her seat, she had asked which way to the Max Palevsky Residential Commons.

"Wait. Don't move," his mother said as soon as he opened the door. His mother said as she stood there with the same proud and beaming mien she had worn to his other two graduations.

Evan curved the corners of his lips for her, but had to squint as the afternoon sun was looking into his eyes. His mother checked the photo on the screen.

"Your eyes are closed."

"It's fine, Mom. Don't worry about it," Evan said as he began taking a few steps toward her.

"Come on, Evan. Please. I want to frame this."

Evan put on a different smile for her like he was changing shirts for her and shifted weight to his other leg.

"Oh, you look so handsome. I wish it was in your graduation gown, but I'm sure you wanted to take it off in this heat."

He bridged the distance and wrapped an arm around her. She put both of hers around him, holding tight the only person she had left in this life, holding tight the only one who really made her rise every morning to meet the day. Evan gave a glance to his watch at the back of her shoulder and then broke from the embrace.

"Why didn't you go on stage? Aren't you feeling well?" she asked while putting a palm to his forehead.

"I'm fine, Mom. I just had to leave. Otherwise, I would have been late."

"Late? Are you going somewhere?"

"Yes, Florida. My flight leaves in a few hours."

"You never told me about any trip to Florida."

"I know. I'm sorry. It was a last-minute thing."

"I don't understand."

"There's a conference out there I want to attend. A math conference. I missed it last year and I didn't want to miss it again."

"Well, okay, I guess. It was just that . . ."

"Just what?"

"Oh, I might as well tell you now. I'm throwing you a graduation party tonight. Even your Aunt Mary and Cousin Alice will be there. They arrived last night. From Seattle."

"Thanks, Mom, but you shouldn't of. You know I didn't want a party."

"I know you didn't, sweetheart. But I'm so proud of you and I just wanted to share it."

"I love you, Mom. Tell everyone hello," Evan said and then stepped closer to give her a kiss on the cheek.

"You be careful, okay?" she said, cupping his face.

"I will," Evan replied.

"Of course, you will."

"Mom."

"Yes?"

"I do know what day it is."

"I know you do, Evan. I know you do," she answered, trying desperately to keep the tears from arriving.

Evan adjusted the straps of his backpack and began to backpedal. He was ten or so feet away and now turned the other way when a question made it through all the other things that were on her mind.

"Evan."

"Yes?" he replied after stopping and pivoting around.

"What about your diploma? I wanted to put it right next to your father's."

"You don't get the real ones on stage. They send them out a week or so later."

"Oh, silly me. I should have known that."

She raised her camera. But on second thought, she lowered it from her eye. *What kind of photo would that be? What mother wants a memory of their son walking away?*

* * *

On the train to the airport, Evan took a window seat in the fourth car. A matter of minutes and it jerked forward. He was thinking about his mother and how lonely that walk from his dorm room to her car must have been. He was thinking about his father and what must have been flashing through his mind during those final seconds. And then, he was thinking about that truck driver sitting somewhere with a gun to his head. The train came out of the gray and sprayed the compartment with the rays of the afternoon. It was a welcome flick of a light switch that eased both body and mind for the rest of the ride.

Evan was already at the doors when the train pulled into the lower level concourse of O'Hare. To Terminal #1 he alternated between a short burst and a fast walk. At the kiosk, he typed in his confirmation number and then typed it once more. This time he was certain that he hadn't inadvertently fat-fingered a stray character. This time he was positive the system was not recognizing the reservation he had made back at campus. Uncharacteristically, he swatted the side of the machine and then stepped in line. While waiting for the family of four currently at the ticket counter, he checked his watch and began to wonder if he just wasn't destined to be on that plane.

"Hi, may I help you?" the ticket agent asked.

"The check-in kiosk didn't recognize my confirmation number," Evan answered as he stepped forward and pushed aside a wave of walnut-colored hair that had fallen too far out of place.

"Well, I can take care of that for you. I'll just need the number."

"It's FWBN55465253AF."

"Impressive," the ticket agent replied, a bit astonished that it was memorized and not read. She smiled and then added, "That's a pretty good memory you got there."

"It's nothing really," he said. "I just have this thing for remembering long lists of data. It's called being a mnemonist."

"Wow, I wish I was one of those. But since I'm not, could you please repeat it a little slower?"

"Sure, sorry. It's FWBN55465253AF," Evan repeated, voicing each letter and number with enough space between so that it would be typed in with no mistake.

"No, I don't have anything with that number. You're sure about it, right?"

"Yeah, I'm sure. Absolutely sure."

"Okay. Just give me your last name, destination, and time of departure."

"Adamko. Buffalo. There should be a 3:10 flying non-stop and landing at 5:40. I know I arrived late, but I wasn't sure if I was even going," he stated, then wondered why he had even appended on that last part.

"Don't worry. It's okay. Just give me a minute. I'm sure we still have seats available. I mean it's Buffalo, and it's June."

Evan took his eyes off of her for a moment and reached into

his back pocket to take out his wallet. He was fumbling through it when she asked him for a driver's license.

"I don't drive. I have a state ID. That'll do, right?"

She looked up briefly to give him a nod of her head.

"Checking any bags?"

"No."

"Okay, Mr. Evan Adamko. Here's your ticket. You're gonna have to run, though. The plane boards in five minutes. I'll let them know at the gate. Have a great trip."

* * *

Evan removed his backpack, set it on the bed, and started to unpack in the slutty Buffalo motel room. As he was removing his clothes, a bottle of cologne fell to the floor. To his knees he dropped to retrieve it, and there noticed an unopened bottle of liquor under the bed. He rolled it forward and saw that hidden behind it was a hypodermic syringe and a spoon. For a moment he thought about changing motels. For a moment he thought about pulling out his phone and catching a morning flight back to Chicago. Both thoughts he was able to defeat when after closing his eyes, an image of his father appeared, and then next the photo of the girl on the Internet.

Clothes unpacked and hung, he walked over to the desk and set up his laptop. He was still on his feet when he logged onto Facebook. A few more clicks and he was at her profile. He took a seat and navigated into her photo album. Three taps on the right arrow brought him to the picture that made him wonder about her the most. She was standing there in what seemed to be a coffee shop. She was standing there as if she didn't want to be photographed. She was standing there wearing her beauty as if it was the last thing on her mind. She had her eyes hidden behind silver-framed, blue-tinted aviator sunglasses. She had straight, pale blonde hair that came to an end a few inches above her waistline. Evan guessed she couldn't have been any taller than five feet five and guessed she couldn't have weighed anything more than one hundred and ten pounds. She was wearing weathered Chuck Taylor All-Stars minus the laces. She was wearing faded blue jeans held to that thin frame by a black leather belt, silver buckle. She had on a body tight, cardinal red T-shirt with white lettering that read: "Keroin Hills, USA." The longer he stared, the more she reminded him of an eidolon or perhaps even a revenant.

He closed his eyes and tried to picture her when she was four. He tried to picture her face just as she was being lifted out of her mother's car and placed into his father's car. He was wondering if she was frightened at all. He was wondering what was going through her mind eighteen years ago, eighteen years to this day.

Without leaving the page and without closing the cover to the laptop, Evan stood up and walked over to the nightstand. He took the framed photo into both of his hands. His father had him held high above his head. His father had on a simple black suit and a simple white dress shirt with a thin tie. His father had on a smile so wide that both his top and bottom teeth could be seen. And just as the salt burn of his eyes began, he started to wonder: *What was I thinking? What was I thinking at that time?*

Evan reached out a hand and turned off the lamp. On the bed

he lay supine and on his chest placed the frame. There must have been a reason for the exchange. There must have been a reason why there's still an Amanda Smith and no longer his dad. She must have grown up to be a doctor, a lawyer, a social worker, someone the world needed desperately. *God, there must have been. Everything is ordered and nothing violates. Everything is ordered and nothing violates.* This thought he had on repeat even after the laptop screen had timed out and the Neptune blue in the motel room faded to a pitch-black universe.

UNIVERSITY OF DISCONTENT – POSTDOC NIHILIST

J OHN CRUSHED THE CAN IN HIS HAND and changed the station on the television. It was his fourth beer since he had awoken an hour before. He was bored with the thoughts in his head and bored with what they were telling him on the screen. He had already left two messages on his dealer's phone and was now contemplating just scoring from the streets. That would have been a great idea except he had only two dollars to his name, and Amanda had once again fallen asleep with her purse safely beneath her head. Another beer he opened and another cigarette he lit.

The idea came somewhere during the commercial break. That TV would have to get at least forty from the pawnshop. He could just say it broke. How in the hell would she know anyway? The TV he had on the floor. The cord he was tracing back to the electrical socket. He was just about to rip the plug right out of the fucking wall when a text came in that said: "I'm Here."

He went to the window and slightly parted the curtain. There below, he saw his landlord sitting on a dragon red Primavera Vespa, dressed in a black suit, white shirt, and a tie. He had his helmet in one hand and his phone in the other. John withdrew his fingers and retreated back to the couch. He quickly finished his beer and then moved on to the last one from the six-pack.

"Come on. Open up. I know you're in there. I saw you," his landlord said after making it up to the second floor and knocking a few times on the door.

Leaning forward, John grabbed the remote to the stereo and aimed it at the receiver. With that, the knocking turned into pounding. With that, he turned up the volume. It was a childish act of impertinence and escalation, but he really didn't give a shit. He stretched his arms across the back of the couch and put on a contented smile. There he would have remained for the rest of the afternoon if his landlord hadn't put his key in the lock and opened it to the width of the security chain.

"Looking for someone?" John said after turning back down the volume, getting up from the couch, and walking over to the door.

"Can you please just take the chain off? I want to talk to you."

"Got a warrant?" John returned.

"Are you really going to be like this? After all the shit I've done for you."

"Uh, yeah."

"I can't keep carrying you. You know that, right? You're three months late on the rent. Again. And the other tenants are calling me around the clock about the noise. Yesterday the cops called me. They said they're getting complaints from the neighbors about all the drug activity. They told me if it keeps up they're going to raid this place and have it condemned as a drug house. I'm not losing this building over you. I've got shit to pay for myself, John."

"Like what? That kiddie scooter you rode up on. Or maybe it's that fucking BMW you just bought. You should really limit your material intake and you wouldn't have all these goddamn problems."

"The only problem I ever seem to have is with you."

"I would think by now that such an outstanding citizen such as yourself would have learned to choose the people he associates with more wisely."

"Yeah, no shit," the landlord replied and shook his head. "What the fuck happened to you anyway, man? Just how does one go from star high school wide receiver to junkie? You had so much in front of you."

"Just for your information, I hated football. And come to think of it, I really didn't like you that much either. You were a dick when we were kids, and you're even a bigger dick now."

"You're going to disappear someday, John. You know that, right? They're going to find you in the gutter and ship you off to an unknown grave. No one is even going to know you died."

"Get the fuck out of here," John said as he stepped back and gave a hard kick into the grain of the door that slammed it shut.

"Two weeks. That's all you got. And those fourteen days aren't even for you. They're for Amanda. How do you even look in the mirror knowing how you fucked her life up?"

That last comment had him rushing the security chain off its track. At the top of the stairwell, he whipped the beer can down and hit his landlord in the left shoulder blade. His landlord stopped momentarily, turned his head to the side, and then continued on his way.

"You come back here again, you better have the entire goddamn police force with you because I'm going to fuck you up. You got that, asshole."

The landlord headed out the door without even thinking twice about the threat. With that, John made a fist and suckered punched the wall. The gypsum offered no resistance at all, but the two-by-four behind it caused him to shudder in pain. He was holding onto his wrist when the apartment door down the hall opened, and an old woman stepped into the frame. Barefoot, she stood there in a heather gray knit robe cradling a rabbit in her arms. She had her long ash-colored hair pulled back in plain silver barrettes the same way she had since she was fourteen. The look she gave him was neither censure nor rebuke. She had no intention of calling the police. She just wanted to see what had startled her rabbit and caused it to shiver and shake while she was listening to some talk show on the AM radio.

"What are you looking at? Get the fuck back inside you nosy bitch," John shouted at her.

The old lady slipped back into her apartment and John returned to his. After deciding against pawning the television, he lifted it up and placed it back to where it had been. And after pivoting around, he found Amanda standing in the middle of the living room. She had her hands behind her back. She was wearing nothing but plain white cotton underwear and a waist-length navy blue hoodie with the writing "University of Discontent – Postdoc Nihilist" imprinted on the front in Syracuse orange. She was there in her bare feet. She had her hair tucked behind her ears just the way that her father adored. The look she gave him was neither meant to antagonize nor reproach. She just wanted to know why his voice, and that of another, had broken into one of her few good dreams.

"What?" John asked as he wiped the sleeve of his shirt underneath his nose.

"Who were you talking to?"

"Nobody important."

"It sounded like Tim."

"You eavesdropping on me?"

"No, John, I wasn't eavesdropping. I was fucking sleeping."

"Well, you can go back to your comfy bed and put your head back down on your purse."

"Yeah well, I would love to put it down on a pillow. The problem is that if I don't sleep on my purse, the asshole whom I live with will keep stealing all of the money I have inside of it."

"That's bullshit, Amanda. I don't steal your money. You just never remember how much you have."

"Okay, you're right. That's exactly it. My accounting skills suck."

"Are we done here?"

"As soon as you answer my original question."

"And that was?"

"Who were you talking to?" John turned his head to the side and sucked his lips. He would have kept his eyes away from her if she hadn't pressed on. "It was Tim, wasn't it?"

"Might have been."

"What did he want?"

"Nothing. Just wanted to see if I wanted to hang with him later this week."

"Are you going to go?"

"Thinking about it."

"So you guys aren't fighting anymore?"

"No, I'm still pissed. But I'm trying to be a little more forgiving in my relationships. Might be all the yoga I've been doing lately."

"Funny. You sent him the rent money last week, right?"

"Yeah, of course I sent it to him," John replied with no glint in his eyes of the lie he was hiding behind.

"Really?"

"Yes, Jesus Christ, Amanda. I sent him the goddamn rent money. Now get off my back."

Amanda gave a start back to the bedroom. For a moment there she wasn't going to give him what she held in her hands. On second thought, though, she weakened as she had always weakened. It was a fault she understood that she carried into every relationship, whether that would be with her mother, Julia, or any boy who entered into her heart. That was something that needed to change, but today that change would remain on her resolution list. She removed the towel she was using to conceal it and then held out the gift.

"Here."

John took it from her outstretched hand. He flipped it over once and then flipped it over again.

"What is it?" he questioned.

"Just open it."

John tore away the Peanuts wrapping paper. Underneath, he found three vinyl albums from three bands that he adored. It brought a slight smile to his face, and inside of her, it brought another feeling of self-loathing. She absolutely hated that she had to end the fight with her acquiescence and a fucking gift. He pulled out one of the records and was reading through the liner notes when she commented on them.

"They're original. I had to order them from the U.K. I didn't think they'd get here on time, but they showed up yesterday."

"On time for what?" he looked up and asked.

It didn't surprise her that he had forgotten. It didn't even surprise her that he didn't even say thank you.

"Nothing. Forget it. I gotta get back to sleep. I didn't get home from the bar until five this morning. We had inventory."

Amanda shook her head and began to walk off.

"Come on, Amanda. On time for what?" he called out.

"Our anniversary," Amanda replied as she threw up her middle finger and continued on.

"Fuck," John said as he combed a hand through his hair.

He followed her to the bedroom door, where he found it locked. He rapped a few taps of repentance of the grain, but she was nowhere near getting up and letting him in. She had already positioned her purse just right so that her head wouldn't feel all of the metal studs that lined the top of it.

"Can you let me in?"

"Just leave me alone."

"I'll run out and get you something today. I promise."

Over to his side of the bed she reached and grabbed the two pillows that were there. One she put between her legs and the other she squeezed like it was someone who really gave a shit about her. She grit her teeth to fend off the tears, and then closed her eyes to disappear somewhere inside, hoping for the goddamn thousandth time that she wouldn't wake up.

* * *

Phone in hand, Evan continued down Elmwood Avenue looking inside coffee shops for one that matched the image on his screen. After an hour or so expired, he concluded his next best shot was to start asking people on the street. The first fifteen minutes of passersby balked at the solicitation with only a glance. Finally, two kids with skateboards tucked under their arms stopped when he asked, "Excuse me, you wouldn't happen to recognize this place, would you?"

"No, but the girl's absolutely smokin'. And her shirt fucking rocks, man," the kid to his right answered after Evan handed him the phone and he took a look at it.

Evan shrugged off the comment and moved his eyes to the kid on his left.

"How about you? Do you recognize the place? I think it's a coffee shop."

"Nah, don't know it. But he's right. The shirt's cool as hell. And she is hot."

"Yeah, okay. Thanks," Evan replied as he took back his phone.

"Advice, dude," the one to whom he had first questioned said.

"Sure."

"If I were you, I'd be looking for that chick instead of the coffee shop. You can get a café latte fucking anywhere. That face there comes once in a lifetime."

Evan watched as they dropped their boards and skated away. He placed his hands over his head and exhaled a long breath. He was getting tired of the rejection. It was starting to remind him of his one short year in Little League when he was trying to sell the world's finest chocolate, and the only sales ended up coming from distant family members. This girl he needed to find, though. So, he asked a few more pedestrians before a woman in her early thirties paused at the question and tilted her head.

"Yeah, I think so. It looks like Sweetness Seven."

"Is it around here?"

"About a mile or so," she replied and pointed a finger. "Walk a little way and then make a right down Lafayette. I think it's right there at Grant."

"Thanks. Thanks so much."

* * *

The woman was correct. The coffee shop occupied the northwest corner of Grant and Lafayette. Housed on the first floor of a Victorian-styled building, the length of the exterior was painted with an elaborate mural, and from the blue-tarped awning hung white ceramic coffee cups. It was both inviting and charming, and he was glad it was the kind of place where she could be found.

Inside, the interior was a perfect match for that photo on her Facebook profile. Tulip-shaped light fixtures lighted the counter from a tin ceiling at least 15 feet high. Chalkboards crowded the wall behind the counter with the fare for the day, and a wooden library table filled the center with two Smith Corona typewriters on each end. In the corner, the middle two shelves of a bookcase were weighted down with Monopoly, chess, and other games. He did a quick sweep of those in attendance, but the girl he had engraved onto his mind wasn't there. So, he moved from the door and took a table with a street-side view.

Hoping that she would make an appearance, he put his phone on alarm for a wait of one hundred and twenty minutes. He then took out his laptop from his backpack and returned to her profile for any clues he may have missed. Seven minutes into his recognizance, two high school kids grabbed the table next to him. He glanced at them and then returned to the screen.

"Specials on the board. The rest is somewhere inside of these," the waitress said as she finally came out of a side room and dealt the menus from the thin waist of her five-foot-eleven frame.

"Thanks," replied one of the students, and then began taking off the shirt and tie he had worn in.

"Hey, Julia. What the hell. I was here ten minutes before those kids," a man at a table in the rear yelled out.

"I work front to back, Ted. Not first to last. You should know that by now. Next time, sit your ass up by the windows."

"You know, I'm seriously thinking about not coming here anymore."

"And I'm seriously thinking of quitting so it won't fucking matter anyway, Ted."

The student was hanging the shirt and tie over the back of his chair when she returned her attention to the table. After a glance at the T-shirt he was wearing, she leaned over and retrieved the menus she had just set down.

"What? What's going on?" the kid questioned.

"Sorry. No shirt, no shoes, no service."

"Uh, we're wearing shoes and shirts."

"Yes, this is true. However, the shirt you are wearing is now on the list of prohibited clothing."

"You're joking, right?"

"No. No, I'm not. Check over there," she said and then pointed to a laundry line where seven shirts hung. "See, right next to the cute Nirvana smiley shirt, there's the one you are wearing."

"When did they start doing this?"

"They," she drew out, "didn't start doing anything. I was the one who implemented the policy."

"But it's a cool shirt."

"Oh, correction. Was a cool shirt. Up until the point both J.C. Penney and every high school kid from Canisius like yourself decided to obtain the licensing rights to a band they don't even fucking know."

"I know who the Ramones are."

"Can you name me three songs?"

"All right, I'll put it back on."

"Great. And I'll give you back your menus. Oh, order quickly. I'm due for another cigarette break soon. And I'm a real bitch if I don't have one."

The waitress sidled a few steps to the right and stood before Evan. He checked his shirt and then checked the laundry line. She coughed out a laugh.

"Yeah, I wouldn't worry about yours. Shirts from J.C. Penney with no band affiliation, while they should be, are not yet on the line. Here," the waitress concluded and set down a menu in front of Evan.

"I'll just have a coffee. Black."

"Well, that should be a hell of a tip."

"I'm sorry. I'm just not hungry."

"Yeah, whatever," the waitress answered and then started to walk away.

"Wait," Evan said, though he knew he probably shouldn't have engaged her any further.

"Yes?"

"Would you happen to know this girl?" Evan asked after turning his laptop her way and showing her the screen.

"Nope. Never seen her."

"Are you sure?"

Without a reply, the waitress walked off to a table in the rear. Evan rotated the laptop back. And just as he was about to tap a finger on the keyboard, it began to ring and up popped Ashok's face.

"How are the Keys, my brother?" Ashok asked, leaning forward across the desk and giving Evan a big smile to go along with his big Indian eyes.

"They're fine. Just having a cup of coffee. Going to the beach later."

"That should be interesting," Ashok replied.

"Why should it be interesting?"

"Because you are in Buffalo," Ashok answered and then sat back in his chair. "Are there even any beaches there?"

"You tracked my phone?"

"Oh, years ago, my brother. Do not be mad. I am just looking out for you. Would you like to tell me what's going on?"

"Not right now, Ashok," Evan said as he watched the waitress set down his cup of coffee at a corner of the table and leave.

"You can tell me, you know."

"Yeah, I know I can. Not right now, though. I just don't have the whole story to tell you yet."

"You're not in any trouble, are you?"

"It's nothing like that, Ashok. I should be back in a few days. I just need to be here."

"Then just be careful. It's a big world out there. Nothing like our campus and dorm room I am assuming."

"I'll call you."

"Okay, that is fine for now."

Ashok was the first one to disconnect from Facetime. Evan tilted his screen three-quarters of the way down, stood up from his chair, and retrieved the cup of coffee he had ordered. He then gave a look at the laundry line and took note of the other shirts that were on the prohibited list.

THANKS, I'VE ALREADY FUCKING TRIED THAT

T HE NEXT DAY EVAN WAS AT THE same table he had previously sat. He was darting his eyes from person to person on the sidewalk. The music had fallen to moderato, but his fingers were tapping double time from all of the caffeine tracing through his veins. He had been there for three hours now, and still, not a single face had passed that brought him back for a second look. This place could have just been a one-time stop for her, he began to think. Maybe he should try a new coffee shop. Maybe he should print up fliers. Maybe he should just forget everything and head out on the next plane. Perhaps the past is the past and it is better to leave all that in its grave. And besides, what if he did find her. What would he have to say anyway? He absently lifted up his fourth cup of coffee when his laptop began to ring. A key he tapped and up came Ashok's face. This time, the Indian

Virginia Austin

boy had his hands folded on a desk and a big grin that showed most of his perfect white teeth. The son of a dentist, he was most proud of that.

"Good morning, my brother," Ashok said.

"Hey, Ashok. Long time, no hear."

"I sense sarcasm."

"No, not at all."

"You are missing me, aren't you?"

"You called me, Ashok."

"Yes, but I did so because I knew you were missing me. We have spent three years together, and it must feel to you as if we are married."

"Not exactly."

"Anyway, my brother, I sent you a few e-mails earlier this morning with the names of places you should visit while you need to be there. Did you have a chance to take a look at any one of them?"

"No, I haven't checked my e-mail yet."

"That is fine. I will tell you about them then. The first one is Iron Island Museum. I think this is a must-see. It was built in 1883 and was first a church, which then became a funeral home. Looks very interesting. They also say it is haunted."

"Yeah, I don't think that's really for me."

"Okay, that is good. My second choice for you is actually better than my first choice."

"Then why didn't you start off with it?"

"Because an article in the *Journal of Consumer Psychology* told me that I should not. It said consumers believe that options placed in the center of a simultaneously presented array are the most popular."

"Ashok, I'm not a consumer here."

"My brother, I actually see it differently. You are a consumer of my advice."

"Okay, what's my preferred second choice then?"

"Are you ready?" Ashok asked as he leaned forward in the chair.

"Yes, I'm ready."

"It is a cricket match between the Buffalo Niagara Colts and the Buffalo Niagara Bolts. They play tomorrow. In Tonawanda. It is exactly 9.3 miles away from you. I myself wish I could be there."

"Really?"

"Well, I would rather see a match between Pakistan and India, but I would also love to see this match. Cricket is the most beautiful game in the world."

"I'm just thinking I'm not going to make that. I watched the game with you for three years and I still don't understand it."

"All right, I have one wicket left. Here it goes. How about Niagara Falls, my brother? It is only 21.4 miles from you. That one you should at least pay a visit. Did you know it was formed during the last Ice Age?"

"Yes, I know, Ashok. To tell you the truth though, I don't think I'm going to have enough time to visit it. I'm really planning to be here for only a few more days."

"That is a shame, my brother. It is beautiful," Ashok replied as he reached off to his right. A second later, he returned to the frame shaking a snow globe that within it had the ship Maid of the Mist sailing close to the Falls. "See."

"That's cute. Where did you get it?"

"Gift shop."

"In Chicago?" Evan questioned.

"No," Ashok said with a face of surprise, "I got it at Niagara Falls, of course."

"I never knew you came here."

"Yes, when I first arrived in your country. A lot of Indians go. Try Zaika Indian Cuisine. They have a great buffet."

"Thanks. If I go, I'll make sure to stop there."

"Oh, I forgot to tell you. Your mother threw a very great graduation party. There were a lot of people there. And I met a cousin of yours. We are going on a date next week."

"I don't have any cousins my age. They're all older."

"Yes, you are right. She is thirty-one."

"Alice?"

"Exactly, that is her name."

"She's been divorced already."

"I was told the whole story. And I said it was his misfortune and my luck that things between them did not work out."

"Did you tell her how old you are?"

"Thirty-one. She said I looked quite young for my age."

"That's because you are, Ashok. You're twenty-one."

"Actually, I am twenty. Double promoted back in India."

"And no one said anything about us going to school together?"

"Yes, of course they did. And I told her that you were a very good student."

"So she thinks you were a professor of mine?"

"My brother, I thought you would really be happy about the news. In a month we could be family."

"A whole month, huh?"

"I sense sarcasm again."

"And again, not at all."

"You do understand that everyone you meet and everything you encounter in your life is not an accident. It is always there for a reason."

"When you put it that way, Ashok, I wish the two of you the best of luck."

"Thank you, my brother."

"You are welcome. And now I have to go."

"Okay. Make sure to call your mother. She is worried about you. She is a very special woman. Can't cook. But she is nice in heart."

"Bye, Ashok."

"Goodbye, my brother."

Evan closed the cover to his laptop and interlocked his fingers behind the back of his head. He hadn't spent more than a minute staring out when he took sight of Amanda passing in front of the window. He moved so fast to stand that one of his knees hit the underside of the table and rattled the cup of coffee about. The spill he dried with a few napkins. His things he gathered up quickly. A twenty he had just slipped under the napkin holder when the café door opened and in she walked. Slowly, he eased himself back in the chair and tracked her as she went over to the counter. She spoke a few words to the guy behind it. He nodded, then left through a door off to his right. And in that moment alone, she turned around to stare at a painting on the wall.

She was wearing a white baseball T-shirt with three-quarter length plaid raglan sleeves. On it, in cursive script, the words: "Thanks, I've Already Fucking Tried That." She was wearing the same blue jeans, the same Converse gym shoes as on that Facebook photo he had been studying for the last three months. She had her hair the same length, the same color, the same part. She had the same blue-tinted aviator sunglasses. And, she was still donning that beauty as if once again she had been forced to put it on. The only difference Evan could see, besides the new T-shirt, was that she appeared even thinner than before.

Julia came out of the kitchen door. By the look on her face, it was obvious that she wasn't expecting her guest. She gave Evan a glance, put a hand on Amanda's shoulder, and then walked her a few feet away from the counter. It was only a moment later that Amanda took the cue Julia had given to her and headed for the exit. Evan hurried his backpack on again. And just as he was about to follow Amanda out of the coffee shop, Julia came right up on his table.

"Leaving?" Julia asked.

"Yeah, I put the money under the napkin holder," Evan returned, his eyes sliding to the window to see if he could spot the direction in which Amanda was heading.

"You sure you don't want anything else?"

"Yeah, I'm sure."

Evan took a step to maneuver around Julia, but she sidled left to block his maneuver.

"I'll get your change."

"You can have it," Evan answered, this time moving left. Julia blocked his path again, no longer hiding the fact she was buying time for her friend. He stepped back and replied in a tone that showed her he was somewhat miffed. "You told her I was asking about her, didn't you?"

"Yeah, I told her."

"Why? I just wanted to ask her something."

"Whatever it is, let it go."

"I can't."

"And that's the reason you should. Because once you say that you can't let something go, it becomes dangerous as fuck."

Evan gave her words only a second of contemplation before walking around her. This time she let him pass, figuring she had given Amanda enough of a head start to make an escape. Outside the coffee shop, Evan stood at the corner of Lafayette and Grant. He gave a check down both streets, but she was already gone. And in all probability, he thought, it would be the last time she would return—at least while he remained in Buffalo.

* * *

Evan's mother was on her side of the king bed. She was sitting up with a book in her hands. Page forty-five read and then back to the inside flap. Page forty-six she went through fast before returning once again to that inside flap. Tonight, those were the only words she really wanted to read, the only ones she cared about. There, some thirty years back, he had inscribed the words that would change her life. A smile came across her face, and the book she slowly lowered into her lap. *God, what a beautiful day that was. God, how I was so uncharacteristically brave. My goodness, what possibly possessed me to walk up to him without even a second thought.*

She had just turned eighteen the day they first met. The football team was practicing on the field, and the cheerleaders were going through their routines on the track. He was sitting at the top of the stands. He was dressed in slacks, a collared shirt, and covering that, a vest. His hair was brushed from the side, unlike the others who had theirs combed in a center part. He had on black glasses while everyone else was wearing contact lenses. The burners had their Marlboro Reds, the jocks had their kegs. He just had himself, and in her eyes, that made him so much cooler than all of the rest. This wasn't the first time she had noticed him. Last year she had him in AP Calculus and she had him in gym class. This year she didn't have him in anything and so had no other choice but to be brave and go up to him. She didn't take the aisle. She used the aluminum benches, stepping on each until reaching the top.

"So, why Illinois?" she said with her head cocked a bit.

"Why Augustana?" he questioned back, the book he was reading still in his hands and his eyes still on the print.

The reply surprised her. She didn't even think he knew her name, much less the college she had selected.

"I don't know. Somewhere to go, I guess."

"How about the planetarium then if all it takes is a guess."

"When?" she answered, maybe a little too quickly now that she thought about it again.

"Tomorrow afternoon."

"We have school tomorrow."

"Yes."

The book he closed and placed on the bench. He didn't say another word and then just left. She slewed her head to the right. She put her eyes on the ground. She stood there wondering what in the heck had just transpired. She shook it off and took the spot where he had been sitting. It was warm, she remembered, as if he had been sitting there for the entire day. She watched as he passed by the cheerleaders without even giving one of them a glance. She watched as he crossed the football field at the forty-yard line and made his way toward the other side. The coaches and the players stopped the play at the scrimmage line. They were yelling all sorts of things, but it was obvious he didn't care. When he finally disappeared, she picked up the book he had left. She thumbed through it a few times before finally starting again at the beginning. And there she saw what he had written. She saw that on the inside flap he had inscribed the words: "The girl coming up here I am going to marry. – Jeffery Adamko."

The phone on her nightstand began to ring, and it sent her Godspeed back to the present. The tears had already made their way down her cheeks, and they had already made their way down to her neck. *Funny,* she thought, as she reached over for the receiver: *Where was I when they began to fall?*

"Hello," Evan's mother answered while at the same time dabbing herself dry with her terry cloth robe.

"Hey, Mom. It's me."

"Evan, are you okay? My God, I've been worried sick. I left

messages on your phone and I sent you a few e-mails."

"I know, Mom. I'm sorry. I've just been so busy here."

"How's your conference going?"

"Good, everything's good."

"You missed a wonderful party. Your friend Ashok sure is something else. He had us laughing all night."

"Yeah, Ashok's a great guy."

"When are you coming back?"

"In a few days, I think."

"You think? Don't you know when your little conference is over?"

"No, I know. It ends in a few days. But I was thinking of perhaps taking a Greyhound up to Niagara Falls. Last week Ashok was talking about his trip there, and I thought maybe it's something I should see."

"That sounds like a good plan, Evan. You know your father and I went there right after we were married?"

"No, I didn't know that. How come there aren't any photos?"

"Well, there aren't any photos because your father dropped the camera over the side of the boat. Boy, the two of us laughed so hard at that one."

In those words, Evan reached over and picked up the framed photo of him and his father from the nightstand.

"Mom."

"Yes, Evan?"

"Dad would have been proud of me, right?"

"Oh, of course, honey. You have grown up to be everything your dad would have wanted. Everything, and so much more."

"Sometimes I think I just won't be as great as him. I mean he did an amazing thing. He must have known he was risking his own life by doing what he did."

It was a thought her son had voiced only once before, and that was when he was nine. It was something she suddenly thought that maybe they should have spoken about more.

"Yes, I'm sure he did. But you don't have to do something like that to be great. Your father just happened to be in the right place at the right time for two other people. Sadly, it wasn't the right place and the right time for him. Evan, your dad always thought we are here for a reason. That none of the steps we take are accidental."

"I just heard something like that," Evan answered in a distant voice, his words barely audible on the other end.

"I didn't catch that, Evan. What did you say?"

"It was nothing, Mom. Listen, I'm tired. I'm going to head off to bed. I just wanted to call to let you know I'm doing okay."

"All right. I miss you, Evan."

"I miss you, too, Mom."

EVERYTHING YOU LIKE I LIKED FIVE YEARS AGO

T HE END OF HER PLAYLIST CAME to its conclusion and she cued up another one. For all intents and purposes, tonight the bar had become her own playground. The thirty-something millennial with the hipster beard who had bored her for two hours about his ex had just left, and now the only patrons remaining were two old men sitting off in a corner playing backgammon and nursing their drinks. Against state law, she lit her emergency cigarette. And against her own rules, she poured herself another vodka straight. To her crossword puzzle, she returned. Forty-six across from *The New York Times* was still giving her fits. *Who the fuck possibly knows the fictional spy who appeared in* Call for the Dead, she thought. That though was the least of her problems as that ache in her body was starting to rise up like it was a Lernaean Hydra. Every time she found a reason not to reach for the two grams in her purse, another two counterarguments she could give for why the fuck not. She pulled her purse out from underneath the counter and was about to head for the bathroom when the door to the bar opened.

Julia walked in and Amanda returned her purse to where it had been. She was glad to see her friend, but at the same time, she was a little pissed at what would have been a well-deserved fix. Julia took a seat on a barstool just off to the left of the five beer taps. Amanda stepped in front of her and said hello with a small wave of her hand. After setting her phone down on the counter, Julia swept a look around the place. Eyebrows raised and eyes widened, she opened the conversation.

"Wow, this place is rocking."

"Yeah, it's sucked all night. Seven dollars in tips. And I had to show one of my tattoos to one of those old men for five dollars of that."

"Which one?" Julia asked.

"Which old man, or which tattoo?"

"Let's start with which tattoo."

"The one near my crotch. Fortunately, I'm wearing underwear tonight, so I don't even think that counts as full exposure."

"It's come to that, huh?"

"Yep."

"I like your shirt if that helps," Julia said as she looked at the jet-black scoop neck T-shirt Amanda was wearing with the words "Everything You Like I Liked Five Years Ago" in white block lettering.

"Nope, not one fucking bit."

"Okay," Julia replied with a roll of her eyes.

Amanda then turned around. She took that emergency cigarette at rest atop the till and brought it with her to the conversation.

"I thought you quit."

"I need to keep at least one addiction around. Lose too many friends at once and then where would I be?"

"You'd still have me."

"This is true. So, what can I get ya?"

"Bourbon."

"Neat?"

"Hell yeah, you guys water that shit down enough."

Amanda grabbed a bottle off of the top shelf. As she was pouring, Julia rotated the crossword puzzle so she could have a look.

"Here you go," Amanda said. "Neat. Just as you requested. Three-quarters bourbon and one-quarter tap water."

"You don't even cut it with Evian or some shit like that?"

"I'll put that down in our suggestion box. For right now, it's just Lake Erie natural spring water."

"Okay, time to toast," Julia said as she lifted her glass. "Any ideas as to what?"

"Not one fucking clue."

"Perfect."

The friends since freshman year high school kissed their glasses. And before the ringing had dissipated, they had their drinks finished off almost simultaneously. Amanda started the refill, and Julia slid the crossword puzzle back to where she had confiscated it.

"George Smiley," Julia said.

"What?"

"Number forty-six across. George Smiley."

"Fuck," Amanda said as she lifted the puzzle to her eyes and realized that the answer was correct, "you're right. It is George Smiley. How in the hell did you know that?"

"My father used to read John le Carré to me before I went to sleep."

"Seriously?"

"Yeah, seriously. It should have been the first sign he wasn't going to stick around."

"Have you heard from him?"

"No, just the same bullshit postcards he sends to me on my birthday and Christmas. I'm glad he's having a great fucking life running around the world. Oh, speaking of great men. How's John? And please, answer in less than two hundred and eighty characters. Last time I asked it took four hours."

"Okay," Amanda began. "Unemployed. Lazy. Fuckhead. Junkie. Asshole. How was that?"

"Good. And now the reason you stay with him?"

"Cause I'm a fucking idiot. That's why," Amanda said. Only a few words about John and already she wanted to get off the subject and stab a needle into a vein. She gave her liver a rest, took a drag off of her cigarette, and redirected the conversation. "Hey, did that kid come in today?"

"No, I didn't see him," Julia replied.

"Why do you think he was looking for me?"

"I have no idea. He seems pretty straight up. Clean cut. I don't think he's from around here, though."

"Why do you say that?"

"I don't know. He just doesn't seem like it. Maybe I'm wrong. Maybe he's from our high school or something. I've had a few of those."

"A few of what?" Amanda asked.

"Guys who like had a crush on me in high school, and now five years later they've finally gotten the balls to ask me out. Total creepsville, though. I mean they were nice guys and everything, but just as weird as they were back then. Fucking Facebook and Intelius. Anyone can find you now."

"You never told me you had guys from our high school looking you up."

"Didn't think it was that important, I guess."

"Fuck, no one's looked me up."

"And now you've been officially inducted. Welcome."

"I don't know. I think we would have remembered him."

"Why? He looks like one of those math geeks who you didn't even realize was there until he stood up on stage to give the valedictory speech."

"If you think about it, those were probably the guys we should have been going after instead of the dicks we did."

"Speak for yourself. I'm single here, girl."

"Uh, if you don't remember, the reason you're single is because Tommy's wife came over to your apartment two months ago and politely asked if she could have her husband back."

"What a fucking dick he was."

"See." Amanda punctuated her last word by tilting her head

back and finishing the rest of her drink. It was a glass she could have done without. It was the one that made it so easy to break all of the promises she had made to herself. It was the one that took an eraser to the chalkboard on which she had written the word "guilt" upon. "Hey," she began, "can you watch the bar for a second? I've got to head to the girl's bathroom before I start bleeding down my leg."

"Well, that's good news."

"That I got my fucking period?"

"No, that you're not pregnant."

"Oh shit, if I were pregnant, it would be God's child. John and I haven't slept together for at least six months."

"Well, that sucks. The best thing for a shitty relationship is always sex."

"Unless you're us. Then it's drugs."

"Yeah, that's worked out well for the two of you, now hasn't it?"

Amanda answered by topping off Julia's drink with the ounce or two left in the bottle of bourbon and then grabbed her purse from underneath the counter. As she left for the bathroom, she thought to herself that she had sold that excuse beautifully.

* * *

Amanda closed the bathroom door and immediately turned around to thread the cabin hook through the eye. She hurried a hand into her purse and began to set her instruments on the sink like a back alley surgeon getting ready to operate. A neon purple lighter from

Walmart. A metal bottle cap from a 40-oz. A sterile-packed hypodermic syringe from the needle exchange program's mobile truck, and a ten-dollar packet of heroin from a friend. She had no guilt now. The liquor inside had already told her twenty minutes before that everything was going to be just fine.

The silver-studded belt she was wearing she unbuckled and pulled through the loops as if it was the cord to a gas lawnmower. Gravity dropped her jeans a few inches from her waist, but her hips hung on to keep them from falling farther. She had the middle of her belt in her teeth when she filled the bottle cap three-quarters with water. She had a good half of the heroin packet sprinkled in when she decided why in the hell not empty the rest. A flick of the lighter and soon began the boil. *All this bubbling in heaven's cauldron,* she thought, and the thought it curved her lips up just slightly.

It was time. And time would soon be defeated. The belt she strapped above her elbow. The syringe she put between her teeth. She pumped her fist a few times, and a vein rose up to draw a nice blue line on the surface of her skin. Rudely, she welcomed its arrival with three hard slaps from the four fingers of her right hand. The tip of the 27-gauge needle she drove through the cigarette filter she had just separated from the Marlboro Red. The cigarette filter she dipped in and began to stir it around. She withdrew the plunger, and the heroin filled up the chamber with more or less one cc.

Everything now in reverse. Plunger down. Heroin in. The elysian rush through her body hit her like a freight train. She inhaled a deep breath and unbuckled the belt around her arm. On the toilet, she repositioned herself to face straight ahead. And just as she leaned back into the water tank, she noticed the cartoon that someone had drawn on the door. She blinked a few times to bring the image into focus. She shook her head to make sure she wasn't imagining it. But there was no mistake. In black permanent marker, it indeed was a picture of Aesop's tortoise fucking a hare that was asleep under a tree. And in black permanent marker, the caption attached to the tortoise said: "Don't worry, it's only a dream."

The heroin grabbed her for the second time, and this time it didn't let go. Finally, she lost control and she began to list. The crash of her head into the wall shook her eyelids closed as if she was nothing more than a child's doll. It didn't matter. She didn't feel a thing. She had already faded away into a glorious state of nonexistence.

* * *

Julia had one hand wrapped around her glass, and with the other, she was tapping out the beat to the music. And as she was staring at the mahogany woodwork in front of her, the alcohol began to drag her nine years into the past. She was remembering the first time she had met Amanda. She was thinking of their first day in high school. Their lockers were right next to each other. *How does fate exactly determine that? How does it know you'd be a perfect match for each other? Assign a locker to either one ten feet away and you would never meet. Assign lockers right beside each other and you would become best friends forever. Funny how that is,* she thought and tilted her head back to finish what was left of her drink.

The first bell had rung and the hall was clearing. Her class schedule that was supposed to be in her purse was in all likelihood somewhere in her locker. She was a skinny-ass kid now on a skinny knee pulling everything back out. It was at that moment she saw Amanda come walking down the hall. She had on ripped blue jeans shredded at the thighs, she had on rose-tinted sunglasses. She had on a black T-shirt, that with a white paint pen, the saying "I SLEPT WITH JUSTIN BIEBER" had been written. She thought the girl was a senior, and so as she neared, Julia removed her gaze and continued searching through her locker.

"I'm assuming they're going to write you up for being late," Amanda said as she parked herself right beside the locker next to hers.

"I know. I can't find my schedule," Julia returned.

"First class?"

"English," Julia replied. "What's it like here?"

"Fuck if I know," Amanda said as she opened her locker.

"Did you transfer or something?"

"Yeah, I transferred from my bullshit grammar school to this world-renowned institution of higher learning."

"You're a freshman?" Julia asked in astonishment.

"Unfortunately, I am."

"You look older."

"I need to bring you to the liquor store."

"You think they're going to let you wear that shirt?" Julia then questioned.

"No, and that's why I'm leaving. I'm just waiting for my mom to pull away. She has this terrible habit of making sure I stay where I'm supposed to be."

"Where are you going?"

"The woods."

"Alone, or are you meeting someone?" Julia asked.

"Just me and *The Idiot*," Amanda said as she pulled the Dostoyevsky book out of her backpack and held up the cover for Julia to see.

"Oh, okay. Then I guess I'll have to smoke this alone," Julia replied as she reached in her purse and pulled out a joint.

"Holy shit."

"Yeah, holy shit."

"I thought you were just some dumbass freshman."

"And I thought you were just some bitch."

"I am. But come on. Let's get the hell out of here."

"Okay."

That day they spent sitting cross-legged from each other. That day they spent trading secrets neither would have dreamed of telling anyone else. Julia had asked why Amanda was wasting time reading a Russian writer. Amanda said he was her father's favorite author. She said after he died, it was just something that seemed to keep him alive. Amanda asked Julia when did she start smoking weed. Julia pulled up a tuft of grass and replied it was not too long after her father had enough of the family life. Amanda answered with: "Happy families are all alike. Every unhappy family though is unhappy in its own way." Julia added, "Love is whatever you can still betray. And betrayal can only happen if you love." And while it seemed like they were just throwing out quotes from authors, both were really just throwing out words from fathers that they missed terribly.

Julia smiled after the reverie. *God, what a perfect day that was. Fuck, you don't get too many of those later on in life. Those are the stories you keep telling yourself when you start believing there's nothing left ahead.* She gave a check of the texts and e-mails on her phone and then stared straight ahead. Solid mahogany, the back bar stretched half the length of the interior. Four Corinthian columns divided it into three. In the middle, the mirror was stenciled "JAMESON" in gold-leaf lettering. To the left and right, five glass shelves. To keep herself occupied, she started counting bottles on those shelves when a backgammon game was set down on the counter just to the left of where she was sitting. Before leaving with his friend, the old man who placed it there then reached into his wallet and put a five on the wooden grain. When she was certain they had exited, she opened her purse and added a ten-dollar bill. *Amanda deserves that. She deserves so much more than that.*

A twist of her wrist and Julia took a look at the face of her watch. Fifteen minutes had elapsed, and now she was wondering what in the hell could be taking Amanda so long. She got off the stool and walked over to where the bathrooms were located. The door to the men's was flung open, but the one to the women's was closed. Twice she knocked. Twice she called out Amanda's name. The knob she twisted and pushed. It opened only to the length of the hook, and now the panic started to metastasize.

"Amanda," she called out again. "Come on, undo this hook. I

swear I'm going to give you ten more seconds and then I'm kicking the fucking thing in."

As said, Julia began the count. Ten though seemed too long, and when she hit five, she stepped back and drove her foot so hard into the wood that it splintered and tore off the piece that was needed. Amanda's head was thrown back and resting against the wall. Her arms were hanging down at her sides, fingers slightly splayed. In a vein, the metal spike was loosely attached like she had been struck with an errant dart. And on her lips, there was that death-blue tint.

"Fuck! Fuck, fuck, fuck!" Julia yelled out as she hurried herself over to Amanda and pulled out the needle. To her knees she then dropped and began slapping Amanda's face. It did nothing though to revive the heroin mannequin that her friend had become. "Just hang in here. Someone's coming. All right. Just hang in there."

Tears on her cheeks, that uneasy feeling like razor blades in her gut, she lifted Amanda off the toilet seat and set her up in the corner. She was at the bar a moment later. She had her phone in her hand. At first, she accidentally dialed 8-1-1 and then had to dial again.

"Nine-one-one. What's the emergency?" the operator said as she had said a thousand times before.

"Overdose. She's overdosed. We need an ambulance. Amherst and Howell. The Underground. It's a bar. Tell them to come inside. I'll be waiting."

"What has the victim ingested?"

"Heroin. She shot herself up with heroin."

"Is the victim still breathing?"

"Yeah, of course she's still breathing. Otherwise I'd be calling the goddamn morgue," Julia responded frantically.

"Miss, please. You need to remain calm."

"And you need to send an ambulance over here immediately and stop worrying about whether I'm fucking calm or not."

"It's already been sent and confirmed by the respondents. They're on their way."

"How long?"

"They're five minutes out. You just need to make sure she doesn't vomit."

"Anything else?"

"Anybody there with Narcan?"

"No, I'm the only one here and I thought she was clean."

"Okay, you want me to stay with you until the EMTs arrive?"

Julia said no and disconnected the call. She returned to Amanda and took her lifeless body into her arms. She had Amanda's head resting upon her shoulder and she was stroking her hair. She was shivering and she was scared. Her mind already had her a few days ahead standing graveside looking down into a hole. The image brought up the alcohol and everything else she had consumed. It took everything she had not to open her mouth and let it all go. The wheels of the gurney she could hear now. She turned around, but not before wiping away that wretched taste from her lips. The EMTs entered. She got up and they took her place. A pulse taken. A few questions asked. Narcan in, and immediately Amanda returned from her time spent with the dead.

"You want to ride with us?" one of the EMTs asked as he was placing her best friend forever onto the stretcher.

"No," Julia answered. "I'll meet you there, I guess."

To the exit but not the ambulance she walked with them. For a few minutes, she just wanted to believe that none of this had ever happened. For a few minutes, she just wanted to be alone. As she was walking back to the bathroom the siren blared, and she put her hands over her ears to drown it out. It still wasn't enough to dampen the sound and so she slammed the door shut.

Her initial intent was to rid the place of the evidence. Instead, her body gave way as if she had been delivered the final knockout punch. She teetered. She felt dizzy and she felt heavy. The sink she took hold of and eased herself down onto the toilet seat. Her fingers she threaded through her hair, where she began to pull until she could feel the pain at the roots. It was a futile attempt to keep the tears from flowing forth, and they began to speckle the floor like drops of blood from a deep cut. She was vanquished. She was so fucking drained. Finally, she removed her hands and with her shirt dried her face. Through the haze she looked straight ahead. The cartoon she didn't think of twice but the words "Don't worry, it's only a dream" gave her pause, they made her wonder. *Perhaps, just perhaps, it really is a dream and I'll soon awake.*

THERE'S ALWAYS SOME BUNNY 4 YOU

JULIA WAS SITTING ON A CHAIR by the window. She had it turned so she could stare out at the world below while at the same time keeping a watchful eye on Amanda. Her fingernails she had already bitten down and now she was chewing up skin. She was trying to remember how many times she had been through this. It may have been the third, but it could have also been the fourth. She was so tired of having her mind and body punished like this. These times, they made her unable to eat and gave her headaches that would last for days afterward. She was sad and frightened. She was confused and she was pissed. It was like they had been dating. In the beginning, she had gotten a lot of good times. But now, it was nothing but a long, painful ride.

"Hey," Amanda said groggily and sat up in the hospital bed.

"How are you feeling?" Julia asked, though she didn't even want to be that kind.

"Like shit," Amanda replied as she flipped her hair off of her face. "What time is it?"

"Almost three."

"Fuck," Amanda said, throwing off her bedsheet and hanging her legs off the side. "I have to get out of here. I gotta work tonight."

"Yeah, I wouldn't worry too much about that."

"Why?"

"Mike texted me a few hours ago. You've been taken off the schedule . . . indefinitely."

"He fired me?"

"Yeah, Amanda. What in the hell did you expect? You were shooting heroin in his bar."

"Fuck," she said, then brought her legs back onto the bed and wrapped her arms around her knees.

"Yeah, fuck."

"You found me, huh?" Amanda asked.

"Yeah, I found you."

"Thank you," Amanda replied after a moment of silence fell between them.

"Don't give me that 'thank you' shit. You lied to me. You told me you've been clean."

"I know. I'm sorry. I was just using a little for maintenance. It was probably laced with fentanyl or something."

"Who gives a fuck what it was laced with, Amanda. That needle shouldn't have been in your goddamn arm to begin with."

"I'm going clean. I swear. I'll get back on methadone."

"Yeah, I've heard that shit before. How many times now? Three, or four? I can't even remember anymore."

"I don't know. Three, I guess."

"You're a fucking corpse in training, Amanda. You know that? And I'm telling you right now. I'm not going to be around when you finally die. You better find religion quick and pray that God keeps giving you chances because you've already used up all of mine. You even think about using one more time and I'm done with you. You got that?"

"Yeah, I got that," Amanda said and then added, "I won't. I swear."

Julia started to close her purse. She wanted to get out of there before she said anything that she might regret. The zipper though wouldn't move past the aspirin bottle that she had taken out and returned a few hours back. With the palm of her hand, she crushed down everything inside and finally got the zipper to finish its ride along the tracks. She stood up, threw her purse over a shoulder, and walked over to the foot of the bed.

"I gotta get to work to pick up my check. If I don't deposit it before five, my rent bounces."

"Julia."

"Yeah?"

"I am really sorry."

"Oh, I left a key on your nightstand," Julia said, ignoring Amanda's repeated penitence. "You can crash at my place until you find a new apartment."

"I can't leave John like that. I need a few days. Maybe a week."

"That asshole junkie is the reason you're like this. Can't you see that? Jesus Christ."

"I know but . . ."

"But what? He loves you? Is that what the fuck you were going to say?"

"He does care for me, Julia."

"Look around. Do you see him anywhere in this goddamn room?"

"He doesn't know I'm here," Amanda offered as an excuse for his absence.

"Yeah, Amanda, he does know you're here. I called him when you were admitted. And then I called him again."

"What did he say?"

"Trust me. You don't want to know."

"Fine. I don't care."

Julia started for the door. She wasn't going to say anything else. She was just going to leave. But this she thought Amanda deserved. This was payback for the last fifteen hours that had laid waste to her body and brain.

"Oh, I have a question for you."

"What?"

"Just something that occurred to me last night while I was driving to the hospital."

"What is it, Julia?"

"Do you want to be buried or cremated?"

"Don't do that to me."

"Why? I mean someone has to make the call, right?"

"Don't. Don't fucking do this."

"Come on, just let me know and we'll never have to have this conversation again."

"Okay, you fucking bitch. You want to play that game. I want to be burned. Just fucking burn me so there's not a goddamn trace of me left. You happy now?"

"No, you don't make me happy anymore, Amanda. You make me feel scared all the time. You make me feel like shit inside. And worst of all, you make me feel ugly for sometimes wishing . . ."

"For wishing what, Julia? That I would just finally die?"

"No, for wishing that we had never met," Julia substituted in, though Amanda was correct.

Amanda kept her tears to herself until after Julia's departure. In all the years of her life, she had yet to break down in front of anyone, and that included her father. She glanced into the hallway. She glanced around at the sterile white walls of her room. She took a quick look at the mulberry bruise on her arm. Finally, she set her eyes out the window, and that's when those tears at last came forward. Out there, it seemed like such a beautiful day. Out there, it seemed as if life was for everyone else except for her.

* * *

For the last half hour, Julia had been walking Elmwood Avenue. She didn't have to pick up her check, but it was the only thing that she could think of to get the hell out of there. A part of her wanted to return to the hospital to say she was sorry for what she had said. The other half wanted to make this the last day she ever saw Amanda again. This decision was still swirling around in her mind when she passed a coffee shop and happened to glance inside. She stopped, redirected her steps, and entered.

* * *

Evan had just filled up the last line of the fourth sheet of paper he had written on. He tore it out from the spiral notebook and laid it on top of the other three. Just as he was about to begin writing on the next one, a shadow fell over the page, and he looked up.

"The coffee sucks here," Julia said as she walked up to where he was sitting.

"Yeah, it's not that good," Evan replied as he shifted a look to his mug.

"Homework?" she asked with a glance to the sheets of paper set off to the left of him.

Evan put aside his pen and answered, "No, I'm just writing a letter."

"Huh, I didn't know people still wrote letters. You mind if I sit down for a second?"

"No, go ahead," Evan said, and then moved his laptop to another spot on the table to clear the area in front of her.

"You're not from around here, are you?" she asked as soon as she sat down.

"Does it show?"

"Well, you do have a University of Chicago shirt on."

"Oh, yeah. I forgot I put it on this morning."

"What year are you in?"

"Just graduated."

"Really?"

"Do I look that young?"

"Let's just say I would card you if you wanted to vote."

"Oh."

"Listen, I only have a few minutes but I—"

"Wanted to know why I asked you about Amanda."

"Exactly."

"She and her mom knew my dad, and I wanted to ask her a question about him."

"What do you mean knew him?"

"Well, he died," Evan said and took his eyes off of hers for a moment.

"Oh, shit. That sucks. I'm sorry. I don't get it, though. What does that have to do with Amanda and her mom?"

"They were the last people to see him. Wait. It'll probably be easier to understand if you read this." Evan reached around to his back pocket and took out his wallet. From a compartment that contained nothing else, he pulled out a folded newspaper clipping and handed it over to her. "Read it. It'll explain everything."

Julia read through it once and then read it over again.

"Holy fuck. That was them?" she said, and then handed it back to him.

"Yeah, that was them," Evan replied, and into his wallet refiled the most important possession he held.

"Wow."

"I just wanted to talk to her. Ask her if she remembers anything about it. Maybe my dad had said something. But now I decided to write her a letter."

"It looks like you're writing her a novel over there."

"Yeah, I know. It's really just a draft right now. I'll probably shorten it."

"Mind if I have a look at it?"

"Are you going to rip it up?" Evan asked as he placed a hand of caution on top of the stack.

"You'd just write another one, wouldn't you?"

"Most likely."

"Then it wouldn't matter what I did with this one, would it?"

"No, I guess not."

Evan removed his hand, and Julia slid the sheets of paper over to her side. After she finished reading, she returned them to Evan, face down like she was turning in a folded hand.

"You don't want me to send it, do you?"

"What address do you have?"

"47 Manchester Place."

"Okay, I'm out of here. Good luck with your letter."

"Thank you."

Julia scooted her chair out and came to her feet. She was a few steps into her departure when she stopped and turned around.

"85 Garner Avenue."

"What?" Evan questioned.

"She moved seven months ago. 85 Garner Avenue."

* * *

The man in the hospital bed looked contorted and thin. He looked twenty years older than the time on earth she knew he had actually spent. To him, she was reading a story she had written from a lined notebook in her hands. It was four pages in length. It was about a little girl who had stowed away on a plane to Papua New Guinea.

That little girl was going there to search for an ancient flower that cured everything. That little girl found the flower just as it was about to be picked. She took it back with her and gave it to her friend, and everything was fine once again.

The man in the hospital bed smiled at the ending, and with a hand like the crook of a cane, struggled to reach out and touch the forearm of the twelve-year-old storyteller who was lying next to him. She didn't cry. She didn't even bat an eye. She just inconspicuously moved her arm closer so her father wouldn't think he had lost the ability to do even the simplest of fucking things.

Amanda slammed the cover on her lockbox of memories. She was sitting at a picnic table staring out at the waters of Lake Erie. The cigarette in her hand she set down for a moment, and from the ground picked up a rock that looked like an arrowhead. Into the grain of the table, she etched in: "Fuck, Dad. I miss you so much." The cigarette she returned to her lips. One long drag and the smoke rolled away like an express train. *Where the fuck is she? Where the fuck is that twelve-year-old girl and why was she so much stronger than I am now?*

Amanda looked at her wrist. The hospital admittance band was still on. A few fingers from her other hand she looped under and pulled as hard as she could. The band stretched but wouldn't break. Again she tried and again the exact same outcome. *Fuck it. Stay on. I don't give a shit.* She got up. She soon left.

* * *

The park was always her sanctuary and her holiday away from all the shit going on in her life. Surrounded by the pure and the innocent, nothing she knew of could clear her head any better. The city lamps with their marshmallow-shaped lights made her feel warm and so much younger. The fort and the teeter-totter reminded her of when she was a little girl and thought of nothing more than how long she had left to stay. The slide and the monkey bars were then the only dangerous things she had to conquer. An ice cream cart, a lemonade, and her father. Four dolphins spitting water. A red, white, and blue rocket ship always there and waiting for her to board. *Fuck, it's so goddamn simpler when you're a child. Fuck, why didn't they tell me that? I swear I would have made sure I never grew older.*

Amanda sat herself down on one of the swings and removed her shoes. No kick of her legs to the stars tonight, though. She had a few OxyContin tucked away but was still feeling a bit too nauseous for any kind of interplanetary ride. She was quite content to just sit there motionless with her fingers wrapped around the chains and her feet buried in the cool sand. Here was nowhere, and what better place to be when you didn't want to be anywhere. She closed her eyes tight and tilted her head back. She didn't need to see the sky tonight. All those white phosphene dots she was now seeing would be just fine.

Eyes open again. Off to her right, a rabbit had come to join her. Mottled light brown and dirty white, it was sitting just a few yards away where sand met grass. Down to her purse she reached and came up with the cellophane-wrapped plastic container she had brought with her from the hospital. The peach slices and slab of meat she tossed aside. The wedge of tomato she wrapped into a lettuce leaf. An underhand toss and the offering landed a foot from her new friend. The rabbit twitched its nose, sensed the danger, and scampered off. *Fine, just fucking fine. I've never needed anyone anyway.*

* * *

In one hand Evan had his phone. In the other he had the envelope, now bearing the smudge mark of a forefinger and thumb. He was thinking he should turn around and head back to his motel. He was thinking this epistle should be mailed and not hand-delivered. He was thinking of the quote from W. H. Auden that his mother had framed in the hallway of their home: "Perhaps there is only one cardinal sin: impatience. Because of impatience we were driven out of Paradise, because of impatience we cannot return." But he couldn't wait any longer. He had waited long enough. He had waited his entire life. *What was she like and why was it so important that a trade had to be made? This girl, she must have been saved to change the world. A doctor perhaps she is going to become. A lawyer for those wrongly convicted, a social worker for those less fortunate, an engineer for the next planetary exploration. This is why some people die and others go on. Yes, it was a trade, a trade that the universe dictated.* He was absolutely certain that there couldn't be any other reason why.

Evan's phone rudely interrupted the thoughts swirling inside of his head and told him in thirty feet to turn left down Garner Avenue. From the other homes he had already passed, he had a picture of the one where she would live. It would be a modest blue Victorian with a veranda. And on that veranda, he imagined she had a chair there that she called her own. And next to it, there would be a cobalt-hued bistro table where she sat her chai tea and laid down to rest the novel she was reading. Most of the time she would be alone. But in the times that she wasn't, her father and mother would be sitting close on an iron-wrought loveseat cushioned beige. Her father would have his face hidden in the pages of *The New York Times,* and her mother, a carbon copy of her daughter, would be penning in the last squares of a crossword puzzle. This, he imagined. This he didn't think was too far off from what he would find.

That left turn his phone asked him to make he made. The change of scenery, though, was immediate from the blocks that he had been previously ambulating. The lawns here were untended, the sidewalks cracked, and the dwellings a mismatch of two-story apartments and single-family abodes. "You've arrived. Eighty-Five Garner Avenue."

As Evan stopped and turned to his right, he thought there must have been some mistake. Perhaps there was more than one Garner Avenue, or perhaps he had the wrong Amanda Smith. The two-story apartment building he was looking at couldn't possibly be the correct address. The siding was patched in different shades of the same color. The wire mesh to the front screen door was torn and slumping forward. The concrete stairs were chipped and badly stained. And even if anyone wanted a glance inside, it would have been impossible as the window treatments on both the first and second floors were pulled down to the sills.

Even though certain he had come this far for naught, Evan made the decision to go up to the door and at least confirm the error. Four mailboxes were anchored to the wall. The two on the bottom weren't tagged at all. Top left, the name Helen Brezinski was engraved as if it had been there all along. Next to it, on a white strip of notebook paper attached by electrical tape, Amanda Smith and John Wilson. *This isn't her. This isn't her. This isn't my Amanda Smith* kept shooting through his brain. The mailbox he straightened out and the envelope in his hand he folded up and jammed into his pocket. There was nothing to be delivered here.

Evan retreated from the apartment building with his head down. He was making a left on the sidewalk to begin his return back when she passed him by. She only gave a glance, but in that glance, something seemed familiar. He didn't look at all, wanting to remain anonymous from whoever was walking by.

"Hey!" Amanda yelled out as she finally remembered the face.

Evan kept moving on, hoping that she wasn't speaking to him.

"Hey, fucking stop. I'm talking to you."

As requested, he came to a halt and slowly turned around. She was in the shadows, but he had studied her long enough to know that it was the girl he had been researching from afar. A part of him wanted to just start running because in his dream of her she seemed so out of place. The other half though wanted to remain because perhaps there was a logical explanation for all of this. In the end, the conflict inside of him didn't matter anyway. In the end, it was her decision to make as she began coming toward him.

"Shit, it is you," Amanda said as she neared to within a few feet of him. "You're the guy from the coffee shop. The one who was asking about me."

"Yeah, I'm the one," he answered, now seeing that she was more stunning than in any of the pictures he had seen. It wasn't even a beauty that could be debated or one that could be dispraised. To him, it was a beauty quite improbable.

"What the fuck were you doing by my apartment?"

"I was umm . . . I was just going to drop off—"

"Drop off what?"

"A letter," he replied.

"Are you a fucking postman?"

"No, of course not."

"Then what the hell? And how did you get my address anyway?"

"I looked you up," he replied, covering for Julia.

"What the fuck for?"

"To mail you a letter."

"Then you should have fucking mailed it. In a mailbox."

"I know. I'm sorry. I should have."

"Did we go to high school together or something?" Amanda asked as she remembered what Julia had said.

"No. I'm not from here."

"Then you're just randomly stalking me?"

"I'm not stalking you."

"Oh, I get it now. My mother sent you, didn't she?"

"Your mother didn't send me."

"Bullshit," Amanda said with venom and conviction. "You're

here to check up on me, aren't you? How much is she paying you?"

"Really, your mother didn't send me. I came on my own."

"For what goddamn reason? I don't even know you."

"I came because of my father."

"Your father, huh? Oh Christ, don't say that your father is actually my father or some fucked up thing like that. Shit, that's all I need right now."

"No, God no. It's not like that at all."

"Well make it like something soon because otherwise I'm going to scream until the cops come and haul your ass away."

"Do you remember when you were four?"

"You remember anything when you were fucking four?"

"No, I guess not."

"Good, then that settles that. Leave me the fuck alone. And tell my mother to stay the hell out of my business. I'm doing fine."

With that, Amanda began to head back toward her apartment.

"Wait, will you. Just wait," Evan said and walked a few feet to bring himself near to her again.

"You were in a car accident when you were four, weren't you?"

"Sorry, you got the wrong girl. I was never in any car accident."

"Your mother's name is Theresa Smith, right?"

"So."

"And she lived in Chicago for a little while, right?"

"Yeah, and? You could have found that out on any one of those fucking intrusive been-verified sites."

"That's not how I know. I swear. Can you please just take a look at this?"

Slow and deliberate, Evan reached into the back pocket of his jeans. He unearthed his wallet, pulled out the folded newspaper clipping, and held it out for her to take. She gave him a look of defiance and kept her arms at her sides.

"Please. Please just take a look at it."

Finally relenting, Amanda grabbed at the newspaper clipping. For a few seconds, she waited. She was contemplating whether or not she should even entertain this guy and have a read of it. It was probably another article about another girl who had died of a heroin overdose. There was a time when her mother kept sending them in the mail. No note. No return address. Just a weekly reminder of another casualty. This was too much, though. Now she had gone too far. Now she had decided to have it hand-delivered. But in another thought, it did seem out of character even for her mother. She wasn't the type to let anyone else in on her daughter's dirty little secret. So maybe, just maybe, it wasn't what she believed it to be. She put her eyes to the print and read through it from beginning to end.

"And?" she said, inside wondering what in the hell this had to do with anything at all.

"That was you and your mother," Evan replied, looking into her eyes to see if it affected her in some kind of way.

"What if it was?"

"You're not even a little curious? I mean that guy saved your lives."

"Okay, some guy saved our lives. Sorry I'm not so thrilled with the news but to tell you the truth, I really wish he hadn't because this goddamn life sucks."

Slowly she spread her fingers apart and the newspaper clipping floated down. To him, it seemed like it was out of a dream. To him, it seemed like she had dropped his beating heart to the ground. He hurried to a knee and picked it up. He was returning to his feet when she spoke again.

"Is that it?"

"Yeah, that's it," he said, now more than a little aggrieved.

"Great. You're gonna stop following me now, right?"

"Yeah. I'm going to stop following you now."

Evan watched in utter disbelief as she turned around and headed toward her apartment. He wanted to yell something out to make her feel guilty and ashamed, but he knew that his father would have wanted him to just let her be. She opened and closed the door without looking back. He sucked down a few deep breaths like he was sucking down his last. No reason. No reason at all he began to understand. The exchange of lives was meaningless. And that thought was the thought that shattered to pieces his theory of life having any sort of ultimate meaning.

Evan began the first of his steps back to the motel. He had his phone in his hand. He was already scrolling through all of his apps looking for the one that would book him a flight back home. Suddenly though, he tumbled to the parkway grass as another body collided with him. Lying on his side, he looked up to see a man in his mid-thirties standing over him. The man appeared a little over six feet tall. He had on jeans and an orange and Navy blue shirt from the University of Syracuse. He had a three-day growth of facial hair, and he was carrying a child over his shoulder. From the pink gym shoes, he assumed it was a girl, and that was soon to be confirmed.

"What is wrong with you? Are you blind? I'm holding my daughter here."

"God, I'm sorry. I was—" Evan began to say as he stood up and began brushing off the grass from his pants.

"Unbelievable, you people."

The man gave a shake of his head in disdain and continued to his car, which was parked only a few feet from where Evan was now standing. Into his pocket the man reached. He then shifted the little girl to his other shoulder to try the pocket on the other side. Evan stepped forward to offer assistance while the man continued the search for his key.

"I can hold her if you need some help," Evan said.

"Yeah, I'm gonna hand my little girl over to some junkie. Get the hell out of here."

"Huh?"

From his back pocket, the key fob was finally unearthed. The little girl he placed into the car seat, where he buckled her in and gave her a quick kiss atop the head. While the man was making his way over to the driver's side, Evan looked into the back of the vehicle. The street lamp was putting the little girl into the spotlight, and Evan could see she was wearing a pink T-shirt with two bunnies sitting on a bench. They had their arms around each other. They had heart-shaped balloons floating above them. The caption in white it read: "There's Always Some Bunny 4 You." To appear brave, she wiped the tears from her eyes and then gave

Evan a small wave. He reciprocated with a wave of his own and then a smile. That smile though was soon to be erased by a hushed but stern reprimand.

"Don't you fucking wave at her."

The man got into the car and the car pulled away. Evan followed its taillights to the end of the block, watched it take a corner, and then stared to the ground in front of him. The last few minutes he rewound. The last few minutes he was trying to understand when he took notice of something that hadn't been there before. Resting on the curb of the street was a stuffed bunny that had fallen out of her hands. He picked it up and rotated it about to see its face. A stitch for a smile, two buttons for eyes. A rose-pink nose and large floppy ears that hung low. A little squeeze of its soft body and his fingers almost touched each other like they had become a centromere. This he surmised must have been from all the times it had been hugged and slept on.

He gave it a pat on the head and then noticed on its front paw it was wearing a white band secured by black electrical tape. Gently he removed the tape and stretched out the band to read the lettering that was typed on it. The print was not what he expected at all. The print read back: "Chisholm Park - Patient - Emily Jones." It made him nauseous, and it brought clarity to what had just transpired. He slid off his backpack and found a safe place inside for the bunny to spend the night.

MY DAD IS A SECRET SUPERHERO

ATOP THE ADOBE RED AND LIGHT gray building, the words "Chisholm Park" were large and bold in Times New Roman font. But from the search he had done the night before, he knew there must have been a study group or two that told them not to add "Cancer Institute." In the morning he had called to confirm she was there. The receptionist who had taken his call was still speaking, but he had stopped listening. Eight, maybe nine. She couldn't have been any older than that. Everything that occurred the day before now seemed meaningless. Here he was chasing the past while this little girl he understood was chasing the future.

Evan found the elevator and took it up to the fourth floor. Artwork lined the walls, and down the halls the parents he passed wore their best brave faces. He was at Room 408 when toward him came running two patients. The one with the black leather choker and tattoo stickers all over her arms tripped and fell as she tried to avoid the boy in the wheelchair. Her magenta wig slid off her head and landed near his feet. He was still on a knee with it in his hands when she snatched it away and said, "I think I'll take that." She wasn't even embarrassed. She didn't even have the slightest tinge of red in her face. She fit it back on and then blew a puff of air that momentarily lifted her nylon bangs. "God, he's so cute" Evan could hear the other one say as they both took off and started running again.

Room 420, Room 422, and finally, Room 424. He was going to leave the stuffed bunny outside the door. He was going to turn around and head straight to the airport. He was going to do all that when he remembered the wave she had given him from inside of the car. *Turn away now and you'll regret this moment for the rest of your life. Turn away now and you'll never be the same.* All these thoughts moved him to the entrance of her room.

"Are you lost?"

"No, not me. I am not the one who is lost," Evan replied to the little girl whose face he had seen the night before. He said to the little girl who over her hospital gown was wearing a blue, yellow, and red shirt that on it had the words "My Dad is A Secret Superhero" revolving around a Krypton crest.

"Then who is lost?"

Before answering, Evan took a few more steps into the room.

"Well, he refused to give me his name, but he did say he was looking for a princess named Emily. Perchance would you know where the princess resides?"

"I am the Princess Emily."

"Oh, good. That's great. Then maybe you are the one he is

looking for."

Evan removed his backpack and took a knee. There he unzipped a pocket and brought out the stuffed bunny. Her eyes opened wide, and a large smile ruled her face like it was Christmas Day.

"Sam!"

"Sam, huh," Evan said as he spun the bunny around to have a word with it. "Well, why couldn't you just tell me that when I asked?"

"He doesn't give his name to just anyone. The whole stranger danger thing, you know."

"Oh, I see."

"Can you please bring him here?" she asked while holding up the wrist that was taped to an IV. "I'm chained."

"Of course."

Evan walked the rest of the distance and placed the bunny in her hands. She gave it a child's peck. She gave it a giant's hug. Never before had he seen such a tender reunion.

"Oh, Sam. I thought I had lost you forever," she said, then looked at Evan. "Thank you. Thank you so much."

"You are welcome," Evan replied, hoping that what he felt inside wouldn't rise to the surface and glaze his eyes.

"Where did you find him?"

"It wasn't I who found him. It was him who found me, Princess. Upon the streets I was walking when he encountered me and asked for a ride to the Princess Emily."

"Really?"

"Yes, really. And persistent he was. For naught another

destination would he let me venture before you were found."

"And here I am found."

She had just finished her words when her father walked into the room. He glared at Evan, but held that for only a few seconds as his daughter held out the stuffed bunny for him to see.

"Daddy. Daddy. Sam is back. He's back."

"I can see that. That's amazing, sweetheart."

"Yes, it is. He asked . . . Oh, what is your name anyway?"

"Lord Evan, my lady," he replied with a bow.

"He came with Lord Evan, Daddy."

"You have to get some rest, sweetheart. We have some tests this afternoon."

"But I want—" Emily began to say.

"Emily."

"Okay," she reluctantly agreed, then looked at Evan. "You will come back, won't you?"

"Of course, kind and dear princess."

"She needs her rest," Emily's father said to Evan, then motioned to the door with a nod of his head.

"I'll be right back, Emily. I'm going to walk our guest out."

"All right, Daddy," she answered.

Evan left first. Her father was a step behind. When they had passed a few rooms, Evan felt a hand fall hard upon his shoulder and knew it was time to stop.

"She dropped it outside of the car," Evan immediately said before her father could speak. He said to hurry in an explanation as to why he had come.

"How did you know where she was?"

"The stuffed animal had a hospital band on its wrist."

"Well, thanks. That was nice of you."

"I just thought she probably wanted it back as soon as possible and I didn't want to mail it here," Evan said. "It might have gotten lost or something."

"Yeah, I got that."

"What does she—"

"Don't you dare ask me that and don't come back."

"But—" Evan started to say, wanting to ask why he wouldn't be allowed to see her again.

"I said don't come back. You got that?"

"Yeah, I got it."

With his head down staring at the tiled floor, Evan found his way back to the elevator. He pressed the button and kept wondering why he was being banished from seeing her. While waiting, he heard a tittering of voices that turned him in the direction of the waiting area. Sitting forward on a crimson-colored sofa was the girl with the magenta wig. She was leaning forward with her lips puckered and down below her sitting cross-legged was her friend. After the heavy line of black lipstick was applied, she smacked her lips like a movie star and flirtatiously rolled her eyes at him. Embarrassed, he glanced away but came back for a second look. She held up a finger that signaled for him to wait. She grabbed the notebook beside her. She took the tube of lipstick out of her friend's hand and started writing. The elevator opened and left without Evan stepping inside. He was looking here and there when she coughed, and he returned a look to her. She had the notebook held high above her head. On it, she had written:

"Room 413." The two fourteen-year-old girls laughed and then got up to run off.

JUST YOU AND ME AND TWO ICE CREAMS

I'M SORRY EVAN SAID AND PLACED the photograph of him and his father inside the backpack he had laid on the bed. Seven days in Buffalo were already enough for him. This was nothing like he had imagined. Life was so much easier on the right side of an equal sign. He swept his eyes one last time around the motel room and turned off the light. When he returned to Chicago, he swore he would stop wondering why anything happens at all and take everything that happens as just probability. There is no interrelationship of distant beings and events no matter what Edward Lorenz said. A butterfly doesn't flap its wings in Brazil, and as result a Texas tornado spins. From now on, he would be an existentialist. From now on, he would believe that all these things that bump into us are merely coincidental.

Evan closed the door and walked to the front lobby. He handed his key over to the desk clerk without a word. On a black iron bench, he was reading through all the texts and e-mails Ashok had sent when the machine gray Sonata sedan finally pulled up. He arose and moved his body to the driver's side.

"Name?" the Uber driver asked.

"Evan."

"Okay. We're cool. Hop in."

Evan opened the rear door and sat himself down.

"Can you move over to the other side, please?"

"Yeah, sure."

"Thanks. I like to see my passengers. I've had a few incidents. Nothing serious. Mostly druggies. They don't seem to understand this isn't a rolling drug den. Every week I pick up a few needles back there. Chisholm Park Cancer Institute, right?"

"No, I'm going to the airport."

"Says Chisholm here."

"Yeah. I don't know. Another driver took me there yesterday. Maybe it came up and I tapped it in by accident."

"Can you cancel that and put in the airport?"

"Of course. Sorry about that," Evan replied and entered the new destination. "You got it?"

"Yep, Buffalo International."

The driver hit the accelerator and off they went. Evan immediately grabbed on tight to the armrest. Buses, airplanes, and trains he felt perfectly comfortable riding in. However, cars always made him feel anxious and disquieted. The driver glanced back with a question but asked another one as he saw his passenger holding on to the door.

"Not locked properly?"

"No, it's fine," Evan replied.

"All right. Just checking. I can pull over if you need to open and close it again."

"Really, it's okay."

"Which airline?"

"United."

"Then United it is. Usually takes about thirty minutes, but I can do it in about twenty if you're running late."

"No," Evan answered a little louder than was required, but lowered his voice with his next sentence. "Thirty minutes is fine. I'm really early. My flight doesn't leave until five forty-five."

"Okay. I'll keep it at tourist speed."

Evan took his phone out of his pocket and held it between his knees. He pretended to be reading through texts when, in all actuality, he was looking at the stopwatch app. He was staring it down. He was watching it count up by the decisecond. And, if not for the driver needing a little conversation, he would have remained silent for the entire drive.

"You coming or going?"

"Going. I'm from Chicago. I just stopped here to see someone."

"It's a shit roll of the dice, isn't it?"

"Buffalo?" Evan questioned.

"Well, yeah, Buffalo. But I meant cancer. My mom was in Chisholm a few years ago."

"How is she doing now?"

"I'm thinking probably a lot better than she was doing before."

"I'm sorry," Evan said, understanding that he meant his mother was now among the departed.

"I was there for her, though. That's all that mattered. Some of the best times we had were when she was fighting it. Ya know, no one understands any of this."

"You mean cancer?"

"No, not cancer. That we understand. It's life we don't understand. Everyone gathers for death. She had people out the door for her funeral. Nobody though gathers for life. It's a damn shame, too. Time is so fleeting, and yet we only pay homage to it once it's gone. Kind of messed up."

"Yeah, you're right, it is messed up."

Evan returned to stalking the time on his phone, but soon abandoned that as thoughts of Emily began to swirl inside of his head. The start of summer and here she was surrounded by scary machines and a hospital floor full of other kids fighting for their lives. At that age, he remembered he was spending all his days at the park pool and his evenings reading in a tent his mother had erected in their backyard. He may have wished for his father now and then, but he certainly wasn't wishing he could just see nine, and if the stars were aligned just right, perhaps ten.

At first, he couldn't understand why her father had said "Don't ask me that" when he started to question what was wrong with her. Now, he realized it was probably so hard for those words to roll off his tongue, especially when he was being prompted by someone he didn't even know. The driver looked in his rearview mirror and spoke. The words woke him from his reverie, and he had to ask for them to be repeated.

"I said we're here. The airport. United."

"Oh, yeah, thanks," Evan said as he looked out the window at all those departures who were hurrying about. He then checked his phone to find the stopwatch app was at twenty-seven minutes and thirty-seven seconds. Was it possible that he could have lost over twenty minutes so easily? *Could there be such a violation of time when you would swear that you were only thinking for a minute or two?*

* * *

At the airport gate, there was no one waiting except for him. He had his head in his hands and his mind in chaos. He lay his body across the seats, but that only brought more unrest than it did calm. Over to the window next. The jets took off and the jets landed, but even that repetition wasn't enough to push out all of the thoughts he had. A short walk to a kiosk and a cherry Coke. A trip to the bathroom to throw some water on his face. A trip back from whence he came just to see where everyone else was going. On his return, he entered a gift shop and wandered about. A glance at the headlines of *The Buffalo News* and a flip through the pages of the number one bestseller. Glo-sticks and Niagara Falls memorabilia, "I LOVE BUFFALO" T-shirts, and a rack of postcards. There seemed to be nothing though, nothing at all that could keep him standing in place. That was all until he came to an eye-level shelf of glass rabbit figurines. They all reminded him of Sam, but she already had a Sam and so he kept moving forward.

Evan was on his way out when he absently hit a basket of

rhinestone tiaras labeled "overstock." He was on his knees gathering all of them up when he finally broke down. The cashier left her spot to come and stand over him, not sure what, if anything, to say. He told her he was okay. He told her he just needed a minute or two. He lied and said the tiaras reminded him of his little sister who was sick and whom he was flying home to see.

* * *

Evan paced the hallway more than a few times to espy if anyone else was inside. When he was absolutely certain she was alone, he came to her door and swallowed a deep breath. She gave him a smile as wide as the universe and set aside *The Little Prince*. He returned the smile and knew that forgoing his flight out was the best decision he had ever made in his entire life.

"Lord Evan. You've returned."

"Yes, to bring thy fair lady a gift," Evan replied and walked a few feet in.

"Have you lost your manners from your travels?"

"Princess Emily?" he questioned.

"Take a knee," she mouthed.

"Oh Princess, please thou forgive me. How rude mine manners," Evan said and then knelt as requested.

"Come closer, Lord Evan. I am ready to receive you and your gift."

Evan walked the remaining distance to her hospital bed. After easing the backpack from his shoulders, he brought out the hurriedly wrapped gift and presented her with it.

"I thank thee, Lord Evan," Emily said and immediately began tearing away at the Peanuts wrapping paper. To her, it was studded with diamonds and made of silver. She handed it over to him and then leaned forward so he could place it upon her head.

"From a faraway land, Princess Emily. I had it made just for thee."

"I shall cherish it forever. You may take leave now."

"Princess?" he said, somewhat surprised.

"Oh, Lord Evan, I am just kidding. Can you please sit next to me? I need you to help me with something."

"I am at your service, Princess."

Evan began to fiddle around with the bedrail. However, he was having the utmost trouble trying to get it to drop down.

"Whatever in the world am I going to do with you, Lord Evan? It may be that all you are excellent with is a sword."

"Yes, that it just may be, Princess."

Emily shed herself of the bedsheet and got to her knees. She then scooched over to the side where he was standing and in one motion lowered the rail.

"Princess, please forgive my failings," Evan replied and sat himself down.

"Yes, yes, you are forgiven. Now please hold Sam for me," Emily said as she handed over the stuffed bunny for Evan to hold. She then grabbed her pink iridescent rhinestone-studded purse from off the table next to her bed. Within no time, she had pulled out a pair of scissors and a roll of black electrical tape. One snip of the hospital band on her wrist and no longer did it seem like she belonged there.

"Hey, I don't think you're supposed to be doing that."

"Yes, I know," Emily replied. "Now give me Sam's arm."

Evan spun Sam around to face him and then spun him back again. Emily took the wristband and slipped it over the bunny's arm, securing it in place with a piece of the electrical tape. She gave one big nod of her head for a job well done, and with both hands, swiped Sam back into her arms. She was holding him close to her chest and was just about to say something when the doctor walked in. She slipped Sam underneath the covers, pulled the bedsheet to her neck, and sat up straight as if she had done nothing wrong.

"Emily."

"Doctor Cole."

"Where's Sam going?"

"He said he had to leave."

Emily's doctor walked over to her bed. He gave Evan one look of acknowledgment before running his eyes over her wrists.

"He stole your admittance band again, didn't he?"

"I can't stop him, Doctor Cole. You know how he is. He is quite an incorrigible one."

"Yes, that he is. And a very good choice of words. He is quite an incorrigible one. Would you like to tell me who your friend is?"

Evan popped up from the bed to present himself properly. He was an inch or two shorter than the doctor whom he guessed to be in his mid-fifties. Combed back silver hair and physically fit, he looked as if he had just come off the set of a television series rather than from the bed of a five-year-old boy who had a little less than three months to live.

"Doctor Cole, this is Lord Evan. He has come from afar."

"Well, Lord Evan," the doctor began as he held out a hand, "it is certainly an honor to meet you. I hope your travels have brought you fortune."

"They did indeed bring me fortune," Evan said and shook firm the doctor's hand. "But no more fortune than to return and find the fair Princess Emily still as lovely as when I last departed."

The doctor stepped forward toward Emily. He was about to remove her tiara when instead, he decided to ask permission first.

"May I take this off for a moment, dear princess?"

"Do you have to?"

"Just for a moment. I want to check something."

Evan felt his stomach knot up as the interplay was now becoming heart-crushing.

"Okay," she said, and Evan understood how incredibly brave this little girl was to hold back the tears as the doctor gently removed her crown and set it down on the bed.

"Any more headaches?" the doctor asked while feeling all around.

"No, not one since two nights ago," Emily answered. "I think I probably just bumped it on the headboard. I'm a restless sleeper, you know."

The doctor placed Emily's tiara back on with tender hands. He then checked Evan's look of concern but gave no expression in return.

"Is your father down in the cafeteria?"

"He just left, Doctor Cole. He had to go to work," Emily

answered.

"All right. I will give him a call. Lord Evan, it was nice meeting you."

The doctor turned toward the door and began walking out when Emily called out to him.

"How were my tests?"

"I would like to run a few more," he replied after pivoting around.

"Well, that stinks."

"I know it does. Oh, and Emily."

"Yes, Doctor Cole?"

"The nurse sees that shirt you're wearing over your hospital gown, she's not going to be happy at all."

"How did you possibly know? I have it hidden under this sheet."

"Because I'm your doctor and I'm supposed to know everything."

"You're not going to tell her, Doctor Cole, are you?"

"Patient confidentiality, Emily. I couldn't say a word even if I wanted to."

"Well, that's good. Because I like it and I think it's going to stay right where it's at," Emily said as she dropped the bedsheet she was still holding up to her neck.

"Just You and Me and Two Ice Creams," the doctor read from off the lime green shirt the little rebel girl was wearing. The doctor said as he smiled at the two bunnies who were facing each other with chocolate all over their faces and all over their fur.

"Yes, just you and me, Doctor Cole. As soon as I get out of

this place. What do you say?"

"You got a deal, Emily. You got a deal."

Upon the doctor's departure, Evan glanced at his watch. It wasn't that he wanted to leave, it was just that he thought she should probably get her rest.

"You're going too?" Emily sadly asked.

"Another land to be conquered, Princess."

"Can't it wait? We already have all the treasure we need."

"The knights. You know how they are. They can never have enough jewels and gold."

"Yes, I know," Emily answered and brought out Sam from underneath the covers. She was once again holding her only true friend close to her heart. Evan stepped forward. He gave a shake of Sam's foot and leaned over to give her a kiss on the head. She gave him that smile again and thought to herself that at least she wouldn't have to say that she had never been kissed.

"I will see you when I return."

"Please hurry back."

It was the first time he had ever heard those words spoken to him, and it was so hard to keep the tears battened down. He was a few rooms from hers when the weight became too much for his body to bear. Against the wall, he put his back and slowly slid along it until he came to a crouch. Through his hair, he threaded his hands and pulled tight. He felt weak. He felt small. He felt helpless and he felt alone. But after a moment, he realized that this was no place to break down. There were just too many faces on that floor feeling so much more.

Evan gathered what remained of himself and stood up. He had

just turned the corner and was heading toward the elevator when he saw Emily's father walking toward him, holding a small pink sweater. Into the lane Evan was traversing, he stepped and blocked Evan from moving forward.

"You're going to come with me to the elevator. We're going to take it to the first floor. And then we're going to step outside and have a little talk."

Evan returned with a solemn nod of his head. He was anxious, and he was trembling inside as the elevator began making its way four stories down. On the first floor, Emily's father grabbed Evan by the arm and led him outside the building. Another twenty or so feet away from everyone else and then he pushed Evan up against the wall.

"I thought I told you never to come back. And yet, here you are again," he began.

"I told her I would come back," Evan replied.

"You want to tell me what the fascination is with my daughter?"

"It's not a fascination. I just—"

"Just what? You just like little girls with cancer."

"No, I don't like little girls with cancer. After I dropped off the bunny, it just seemed like she needed a friend."

Emily's father thought about the answer for a moment as he searched about the eyes of the kid in front of him.

"Well, she doesn't need any friends. She has me and that's enough. And she certainly doesn't need a junkie as a new friend."

"Why do you think I'm a junkie?" Evan asked, quite surprised at the accusation.

"Everyone who goes to that apartment is a junkie. You think I'm an idiot?"

"I've never been up there. I was just looking for a girl who lives there."

"Amanda?"

"Yeah, Amanda. She—" Evan began to explain but had his answer abruptly severed.

"Besides her shithead boyfriend, she's the biggest junkie in this town. And somehow, you're the only one in Buffalo who doesn't know that?"

"I—"

"My daughter is off-limits. There's nothing good that will ever come out of her having a relationship with you. I think you're a liar. I think you're an addict. And I think her heart will just get broken. And right now, you are the last thing that should be on either of our minds."

"Okay. I won't come back."

"Good. Now get the fuck out of here."

With those the last of his words, Emily's father grabbed hold of Evan's shoulders and then gave him a push in the chest to get him on his way. A few steps into his departure it struck him how much of an idiot he had been. A graduation he had missed. Ashok he had started to ignore. His mother he had basically ditched. And all for a girl who had taken her second chance at life to grow up and become a heroin addict. His walk became a trot and that trot became a full sprint. Across a park and a cut through a grocery lot, down avenues and streets he had no familiarity with, he kept running. Finally, he came to a stop because his lungs wouldn't let him go any farther and he had no destination anyway. He put his hands atop his head and while catching his breath, began to slowly spin about. In every direction, the world seemed infinite. But for the first time in his life, he had absolutely no idea which way he should head.

APPARENTLY, I ONLY SLEEP WITH ASSHOLES

I T HAD BEEN ALMOST TWO DAYS since his last score, and now his body was rejecting its own existence with everything that it had left. Walking from room to room was now a feat as the muscles in his legs were being besieged by constant cramping. Inside of him a cold front had settled in, but it was hard to tell as every minute or so he was wiping away the sweat from his forehead. The Jack and Coke that he poured when he awoke was presently being splattered across the bottom and sides of an American Standard. He lifted a used bath towel from the floor and wiped his mouth of what vomit remained.

John flipped the hair off his face and exited the bathroom. His first stop was the thermostat, where he turned it up another four degrees to eighty-three. He then returned to the kitchen. This time the search he would conduct would be without the slightest thought of it being a covert operation. This time he would go in like a wrecking ball. Boxes of food he pulled out from the shelves above the countertop and tossed to the floor. Cans he pitched into the sink with no regard. When that still turned up nothing, he got to his knees and started removing the pots, the pans, and the modular plastic containers.

Amanda woke to the discordant sounds of clanging metal and slamming drawers. She woke in a sweat with the bedsheet sticking to her body like papier-mâché. After peeling off the coverlet, she put her feet to the floor and removed her T-shirt and underwear. From the dresser drawer, she used one shirt to pat herself dry and another one to fit over her head. The light brown shirt with lava-colored Kunstler script she thought was the best one yet. On it, she had them print: "Apparently, I only sleep with assholes."

Out in the hallway, she switched the thermostat from heat to cool and set the temperature down to sixty-six. Now in the kitchen, she found him sitting cross-legged, hands interlocked over his head. She found him there like a child who had just emptied all of his toys from a playroom storage chest. She was in no mood to be polite and in no mood to humor him today.

"What the fuck are you doing, John? I'm trying to sleep," she said.

"Where is it?" he asked, hands still interlocked over his head and eyes still staring blankly at the floor.

"Where's what? Christ."

"We had two grams and now there's nothing left. Did you shoot it all?"

"No, I didn't shoot it. Why don't you text one of those whores you had over last night and find out where the hell it went?"

"Those weren't whores, Amanda," he answered while looking sideways. "They were just a couple of photographers I met."

"Well, I hate to be the first to tell you, but they lied on their résumés."

John grabbed the top of the counter and came to his feet.

"It's gotta be here somewhere, Amanda. Come on, help me look."

"I'm fucking tired, John. And so what if I did, it's my money anyway that pays for it."

"Every goddamn time you gotta bring that up, don't you?"

"I wouldn't bring it up if you had a job."

"Fuck you, Amanda."

The expletive had barely dissipated into the air when another idea popped into his head, and he went over to the refrigerator. There was hardly anything in it except eggs, milk, and brown-leafed lettuce. He was just about to close the door when he opened it wide again and took out the carton of eggs. The top he had just lifted when she screamed at him.

"Will you stop it for fuck sake!"

After setting the carton down on the counter, he decided on another approach. He walked over to her and cupped her face with his hands. She recoiled a bit, but he held on.

"Listen. I'm sorry. All right. I just need a little. I'm not feeling good right now."

"Christ, John. You gotta quit," she replied with just a little bit of empathy to what he was going through.

"I will. I swear. For the both of us. You know I love you. God,

I love you."

His words weakened her more. They seemed to come from his heart. They seemed to have been delivered with sincerity. She fell forward into his waiting arms. He grabbed her tight and put her head to his chest. She was caressing his back when he moved his mouth to her ear and whispered into it.

"Fifty dollars. It'll be the last time."

Amanda eased herself out of the embrace and felt like a complete idiot. She went straight to her bedroom and then straight to her purse. This would be easier. The money she would give him would be a down payment on their breakup. She would bring this memory to recall as she was walking out the door. A moment later she returned to the kitchen and handed him her last check from the bar.

"Here."

"You didn't sign it," he said after flipping it over.

"You know how to sign my name, John. You've done it hundreds of times. The only difference is that today you at least bothered to fucking ask."

He was out of the kitchen without even a kiss goodbye. The front door she could hear open and slam. That would be the last knife to the heart she swore, like she had sworn hundreds of times before.

* * *

Amanda woke again. The two OxyContin and three Sominex she took after he left had given her a good morning, afternoon, and early evening rest. She gave the apartment a quick walk-through. He hadn't returned and most likely wouldn't for at least a while. Her best guess was that he had found a way to the city of Niagara Falls. It was always an easy score. Just behind the 7-11 down on Fourth Street, the drugstore was always open and always well inventoried. He would shoot it there, crash for the night, and the next day make the 21.4-mile trip back home.

With a bottle of vodka in one hand and a spotted glass in the other, she took her body to the couch. She poured herself a drink and then reached over for the pack of cigarettes that rested on the table next to her. She really didn't have a taste for either the alcohol or the nicotine. However, addictions she understood, they have to be evicted one at a time, or all of them are going to end up staying like uninvited guests. John had long left her thoughts. He was on his own for all she was concerned. Like she had predicted after their first kiss, they had walked their relationship from lovers to houseguests and now finally to cellmates. In the end, he'd be sorry and she'd be free. So she thought once again.

But though she was at rest, her mind was still in motion. That kid with his newspaper clipping kept replaying in her head. *How was it possible that an event like that could escape the oral history of our family? If it was true, then fuck how nice to just edit and splice like that.* She did a search on her phone, but nothing turned up. He must be lying, but how in the hell does one produce a story in newsprint. Ten numbers she dialed in, but it took her more than five minutes to send.

Amanda's mother was sitting up in bed, an uneven stack of photo albums occupying the empty space to the left of her. She had the television tuned to her favorite show. She had a deck of three-by-fives in her hands. Each one she could remember as if it had just been taken that very day. The phone on her dresser began to ring. She slid her reading glasses down the bridge of her nose and checked the number. "God, what a great photo," she said aloud and brought the picture closer to her face. *Birthday number six. Tiara and princess dress. Cake at the corners of her lips. What a happy little girl.* The toll of the phone died out, and no more than five minutes later, it began to ring again. She set down the photos and reached for the remote. The volume she raised. *This is such a good show. God, how I love hospital dramas.* But on the third ring, she knew it had to be answered. And so, with a trembling hand, she reached over to her nightstand.

"Hello."

"Hi, Mom. Did you just get in?"

"No," her mother answered, and as she glanced at her hand, she could see it was no longer shaking in tremolo.

"Were you out on the patio?"

"No, I wasn't on the patio."

"Then why didn't you answer? I've been calling for the last ten minutes."

"Because I saw it was your number."

"What the hell, Mom. Why wouldn't you answer if you knew it was from me?"

"Because there are only two reasons for me to receive a call from your number, Amanda. One is that you need money, and the other is someone calling me from your phone to tell me you're dead."

"Well, it's your lucky day then, Mom. I'm not calling from the grave, and the living version of myself doesn't need money. I'm just calling to ask you something."

"Okay, then ask me, Amanda."

"Were we in a car crash when I was four?"

"Who told you that?"

"It doesn't matter. Is it true? Were we in a car crash?"

"Yes, back when we lived in Chicago."

"And some man saved us?"

"Yes, he did."

"Why didn't you ever tell me that?"

"You were there. What did I have to tell you?"

"I was four. What the hell would I possibly have remembered about it?"

"Nothing, I hoped."

"Maybe I would have wanted to thank the family when I got older. Did that ever cross your mind?"

"No, it didn't cross my mind, Amanda. And believe me, I tried to thank them. Over and over I tried. The wife of that man just didn't want to see me."

"I just wish you would have told me."

"Would it have made any difference?"

"Yes. Christ, yes. It would have given me . . . Fuck, why do parents shelter their kids from things that maybe they needed to know or things maybe they needed to see? Dammit, Mom, don't you know. Everything might have turned out differently if I was told."

"Then because I didn't tell you about something when you

were four years old, that's the reason you . . ."

"Became a junkie, Mom. You can say it. Your daughter's a junkie. And no, you're not to blame. I have a problem. I know that. But I'm sick. And no one understands it. Not even my own mother. But you know what, if I do die, just tell everyone that I had some rare disease. That's something everyone can understand. That kind of death they empathize with. Junkies, though, when we die, it just makes the world a goddamn happier place, doesn't it, Mom?"

"Amanda. Amanda."

The call she disconnected and gave a fastball toss of her phone into the center of the Christmas tree. The glass she had set on the coffee table she found too far out of range so she grabbed the bottle of vodka between her legs and tilted her head back. It slashed and burned its way down her throat and made her stomach queasy. That didn't matter, though. Once again, she took the devil's trade. She took the peace of mind for a body in pain.

Amanda's mother regretted only the conversation though not the call. Her daughter may have been angry, but at least she wasn't slurring her words or speaking as if her voice had been slowed to half its normal speed. Those thoughts she quickly threw aside and reached for the photo album. There were pictures of that day, and she knew exactly where to look.

The photo album back in her hands, she flipped to the beginning that began eighteen years back. A pose of her daughter in a starfish-patterned bikini near a sandcastle. A shot at the edge of the water. Arms around a golden retriever who had wandered over. An orange-smeared face from a large bag of goldfish crackers. Pink flamingo floatie around her waist. Dead silver fish in her hand, which soon after was immediately confiscated. Holding hands with a new little friend. Floppy straw hat and large white-rimmed sunglasses. And then, then finally the last of the photographs. The one that always haunted her. No one in the frame. Just three little sand angels and the word "Amanda" written by the precocious girl who could already read and spell.

The black clouds she remembered were rolling in north to south. *Odd,* she thought, *they usually arrive south to north on a summer day.* A lightning strike of the sky and then a sonic boom that sent everybody on North Avenue beach running for cover. She gathered up all of the toys and then her four-year-old daughter. To the car they ran, but the hard rain had already beaten them to it. All the accouterments of their beach party she emptied into the trunk and then dried off her little girl before placing her in the car seat.

On I-294, the rain was quicker than the windshield wipers. She checked the rearview mirror for just a second. Her precious cargo was fast asleep. Her precious cargo had her little head off to the side with her arms holding a sand pail, rake and shovel inside. *What a magical day,* she thought. *We need so many more of these.* When she put her eyes back on the tollway, it was already too late. And though she slammed on the brakes, she skidded into a car that was oddly at rest in the middle lane.

Fortunately, the collision was only a minor infraction that wasn't even enough to deploy the airbags inside. She turned around to have a look at her daughter. She reached out an arm to touch one of the little girl's legs and asked: "Are you all right, sweetheart?" The little girl nodded her head. She was gripping tight the steering wheel. She was watching the cars flying by in the other lanes. She had no idea what to do next when at her window appeared the man from the car she had just struck. He motioned for her to roll it down, and when she did, the rain entered the car at the same time his voice did.

"Are you all right?" he asked and then noticed Amanda in the back. Amanda gave him a smile and then a small wave of her little hand as she watched the rain pelting his face.

"Yes, we're fine," she answered him.

"Good. I'm so sorry."

"Are you stalled?"

"No, the car in front of me is. I ran into him a minute ago." She looked through the windshield and realized that this was the second accident. "We should get you and your daughter into my car. It'll be safer. Someone else might run into you."

"Okay," she replied.

She exited, and he had already opened the back door with her precious cargo over his shoulders. He nodded for her to get into the passenger's seat of his car, but she remembered she didn't get in immediately. She wasn't going anywhere until her daughter was safely placed into the backseat. Her eyes though were drawn away as the horn of a semi-trailer began to blare. She could see its enormous grill getting closer. She could see its front wheels were locked and white smoke was rising up. She could see the look of horror upon the trucker's face.

It was all so surreal after that. In a flash, the eighteen-wheeler struck her car as had been forewarned. In a flash, it veered to the left. In a flash, the man standing was there and then he wasn't. The cab twisted first and the trailer next. On its side it slid a little longer, side-swiping cars before finally coming to rest.

The collision had crushed the back of her SUV, and the carom had spun his car three hundred and sixty degrees around. She remembered she was surprised she was still standing unharmed and unscathed. She remembered she was opening the backdoor of the man's car, selling her soul to the very first taker. That man though, that beautiful man, he had been able to place her little girl inside on what she assumed was probably his very last breath. Around her daughter, she wrapped her arms and held her tighter than she had ever held her before. If there were another collision to come, then at least they would get to the other side together.

At the wake, the lines were out the door with relatives and students from the school at which he taught. The visitation the funeral director had to extend by another two hours just to accommodate all of those who had come to pay their respects. She remembered she knelt at the casket alone. It was closed but atop was a framed photograph of him, his wife, and a boy who seemed to be no older, no younger than that of her own daughter. A prayer to God for his soul, and then a thank you to him for saving both of their lives.

"We should go," she said to her husband.

"Come on, pumpkin, it's time for us to go home," her husband relayed to their daughter who was sitting next to him.

"I don't want to go, Daddy."

"Did you talk to her?" her husband asked as he stood up from the sofa and brushed a hand down the front of his suit coat to remove the wrinkles that had settled in.

"No, I tried. But she seemed to keep moving away from me."

"Did she know who you were?"

"I'm pretty sure."

"Maybe you should have taken you know who with you," her husband said as he nodded over to their daughter.

"I didn't want her up at the casket. There's a photograph of him atop of it, and she might have remembered his face from the accident."

Her next recollection was breaking from the sidebar with her husband and crouching before the sofa. The two children sitting there each had a car in their hands. The little boy was racing his back and forth across the backrest. The little girl was right behind in hot pursuit. Even though his face was in profile, the little boy looked so familiar to her.

"We have to leave now, Amanda," she addressed her daughter.

"We're still playing."

"Do you want to tell me your new friend's name?"

Without a look, her daughter gave a shrug of her shoulders, and so she decided to inquire herself.

"What's your name?"

"Evan," the little boy turned and politely replied. The little boy, who sitting there in his black suit and tie, looked more like a little man.

"Where are your mommy and daddy?" she then asked.

It was all so strange after that. The little boy pointed toward the front of the funeral home at the same time her daughter took the opportunity to T-bone the car that he had set down on the cushion. The toy skirted off the sofa and hit her in the knee before falling to the floor. As she went to pick it up, that face she remembered. That face was the same one in the frame she had just seen atop the casket. That boy she now realized was the son of the man who had saved their lives just days before. Immediately, she got to her feet and hurried out of the funeral home. She remembered she made it only halfway to the car before having to stop and vomit. She remembered she couldn't even get the cigarette to light as her body and hand were trembling as if she was standing unclothed and alone on the plains of a tundra.

Amanda's mother needed more than her fingertips, and so she used the edge of the bedspread to dry her face. *Why? Why did I never tell you? The reason is so simple. I kept it from you so I could bear all the pain, you ungrateful thing.* The photos from that day she began to tear into pieces. *Good, I'm glad you know. Now you've inherited all of this, and I, I have nothing to remember anymore.*

* * *

Evan was lying on the bed in the same room he had checked out of earlier that day. He was supine and the room was unlighted. Even though utterly exhausted, he still couldn't seem to fall asleep. He had lain down at ten p.m., but now it was a little past twelve. Things in motion tend to stay in motion, and this he began to understand applied not only to objects but to all of the thoughts inside of one's head. One girl he never wanted to think of again, and the other he had been banished from. What if he had never left? What if instead he had gone up on stage and taken that diploma into his hand? He knew better though than to keep thinking of events that could never be changed. He had been through that exercise many times before and settled into agreement with Hawking's chronology protection conjecture: There is no travel back. The laws of physics are such that they preclude overturning such regrets. In the end, the past is irrevocable and there's nothing we can do to change that.

He put his legs to the floor and walked over to the desk. After opening his laptop, he typed in a few strokes. Ashok's face immediately appeared on the screen, a textbook in front of him and a University of Chicago cup to his right.

"Oh, my brother, it is good to hear from you. We were just about to come on a plane and see you."

"You and my mother?" Evan asked.

"No, why would I be flying to Buffalo with your mother?" Ashok said with wonderment. "Me and your cousin Alice. We are worried about you."

"Why would you and my cousin be getting ready to come out here?"

"Because, as I said, we are worried about you."

"That part I got, Ashok. By why would you be coming with Alice?"

"Oh, that is right. I have not told you. We are quite serious. And when I said I was thinking of going out to Buffalo to check on you, she said she did not want me to go alone."

"She was going to fly in from Seattle?"

"Why do you say Seattle?"

"Because that's where she lives."

"Oh, not anymore, my brother. She has moved to Chicago."

"Where is she living?"

"In our dorm room."

"Our dorm room?"

"Yes, I hope you are not upset. But you have graduated, and I assumed you would no longer be in need of your bed."

"I thought you were just taking her out on a date."

"Yes, I did. And now, she is here. The events have unfolded fast. She is the woman of my dreams."

"You know you say that about every girl you meet, right?"

"I am aware of my past statements. But she is the real thing. The others not so much."

"Is she there now?"

"Yes, she is sleeping, though."

"Just be careful, Ashok. I don't see this ending well."

"My brother, you have people come into your life shockingly and surprisingly. You have losses you never thought you'd experience. You have rejection and you have to learn how to deal with that and how to get up the next day and go on."

"Is that another quote from Tagore?"

"Hah, who can possibly understand that Bengali. It is Taylor Swift. Anyway, how are you doing? Do you have your whole story yet?"

"No, what I have is a story about someone my father once saved, and another story about a little girl I met who has cancer. That someone whom my father saved does not seem to care that my father died to give her life. And as for the little girl, I've been told I can no longer keep her as my friend. I just don't know what to do. I don't want to come home and I don't want to stay. What do you do when you're stranded in the middle of yourself?"

"I am not sure, my brother. But I do know that you cannot cross the sea by simply staring at it."

"Another quote from Miss Swift?"

"No, that one is from Tagore."

"All right. I'm going to go. Sorry I called so late."

"It is no problem. I plan on staying up anyway and keep reading this book on classical mechanics," Ashok said as he lifted up the text in his hands and showed Evan the cover.

"I thought you were taking Quantum Field Theory for the summer."

"Yes, I am, my brother. However, I cannot seem to sleep lately and this one seems to be much better for my insomnia."

"Well, you have fun with that, Ashok."

"My brother."

"Yeah, Ashok?"

"I am sorry these things are happening to you. You are a good soul."

I HATE MY MOTHER
AND I WANT TO DIE

A MANDA WALKED INTO THE COFFEE shop and took a seat at the counter. She was donning a gray and yellow T-shirt with a wasted smiley face on it. She had it imprinted with the saying: "I Hate My Mother And I Want To DIE." The guy beside her in his pitch-black slim-fit Kickstarter pants, white crewneck tee from Anatomica, and lightweight charcoal ASOS cable cardigan turned and gave it a read-over. He nodded to her a smile of approval. She returned it with a look of disdain. *What the fuck did his millennial ass know about the life he was pretending in?* she thought. He went back to typing on his phone, and she put her eyes on the new waif girl behind the counter with the nose ring and sleeve tattoos.

"Is Julia working today?"

"No, she's off. Anything else?" the girl returned with her own look of contempt.

"Yeah, I'd like a coffee, black. If it's not too much trouble."

"You got money for it?"

"Yeah, I've got fucking money for it. Did you ask this guy if he had fucking money before he ordered the avocado toast and side salad?"

"No, I only ask the ones who skip out on their tab."

"What the hell are you talking about?"

"Two weeks ago, you and some guy stopped in here. Ordered breakfast and then took off."

"Shit. I'm sorry," Amanda replied, somewhat penitent. "I don't even remember. We were pretty hungover."

"No, you weren't hungover. You were loud. You were rude. You were obnoxious and you were definitely wasted."

"Yeah, okay. You were there. That's fucking great. I obviously wasn't though. So, how much?"

"Twelve dollars and forty cents. Not including tip."

Amanda dug a hand into a pocket of her jeans and set a laundry-washed ten-dollar bill on the counter.

"That's a ten."

"Yeah, I know it's a fucking ten. Christ, give me a second, will ya."

After finding nothing in her other front pocket, Amanda stood up. A handful of quarters she pulled out and set on the counter. She was stacking the coins four to a pile and pushing them over.

"How much is the coffee?"

"Two fifty."

"Well, there you go. Fifteen dollars. The tip's in there."

"Ten cents?"

"Wow, I'm impressed. Looks like you double majored, huh?

Waitressing and mathematics. Just where in the hell did you find the fucking time?"

"If Julia wasn't friends with you, I'd throw you right out of here."

"Yeah well, she is. So get my coffee, will ya."

After the waitress left, a new song came on over the cafe speakers, and Amanda began a slow sway to the guitar strum. She had John on her mind, she had a flicker of a future that could have been. She had the lyrics forming silently on her lips until she gave life to the line: "And baby when I'm home, big deal, I'm still alone." The sound of her own voice startled her, and she turned around to see Evan entering through the door. She tracked him to the table and watched as he unloaded his laptop from his backpack. The song she let have a few more bars before getting up and walking over. Evan had just flipped up the laptop screen when Amanda pushed it back down.

"I thought you were going to stop following me."

"I didn't even know you were here," Evan replied with a look of surprise.

"Yeah, right."

"Fine, if you don't believe me, I'll leave."

"Good," Amanda answered and watched as Evan swiped his laptop from the table and knelt to the floor. He was unzipping his backpack when she spoke again. "My mother tried to talk to your mom after the accident. She didn't want to talk to her, though. That's why you're out here, right? You were looking for one of us to say thank you, weren't you?"

Evan stood up, threw his backpack over a shoulder, and looked at her green eyes for the first time. He didn't hold onto them too long, though. That bewitch of emerald he no longer wanted a part of.

"No, that's not the reason I came out to Buffalo."

He took a step to his right to take leave. She sidled left to block his escape. With a shake of his head, he rerouted around the other side of the table and now had a clear path to the door. For a moment Amanda stood there undecided. As she glanced over to where he had been sitting, she found that in his rush to depart, he had forgotten to take his phone. She took it from the table, put it in her pocket, and appropriated it for her own.

Evan was halfway down the block when she exited the café. She caught him at the corner and once again stood in his way. This time he stopped and waited for what she had to say.

"Then, why? Why in the hell did you come out here?"

"You really want to know?" he asked.

"Yeah, I want to know why all of a sudden some guy keeps showing up everywhere I happen to be," Amanda said as she flipped back the errant strands of blonde hair from her face that the wind had placed there.

"I came out here to see what kind of person you've become," Evan began, ready now to draw a little blood. "I wanted to know why it was so important for my father to die saving you. I figured it must be because you were going to grow up and become some important doctor or something. Someone who the world needed. But I already found out yesterday. You're a heroin addict. My father died to save a junkie."

"Fuck you. You're an asshole," Amanda answered in the only

way she could after being cut. "And of all the assholes I've known in my short and unimportant life, you've just moved to the top of the goddamn list."

"I don't care about any of your lists."

"Why the fuck me? Why not my mother or the truck driver who ran into your father? Why don't you stalk them like you're stalking me? I can save you the effort on my mother, though. She turned into a bitch who gave up on her daughter at age twelve. The truck driver, who knows. Maybe he turned in his commercial license, went straight into med school and became a distinguished man of the medical community who now works for *Médecins Sans Frontières*."

"The truck driver's dead," Evan replied.

"Let me guess. It was irony that killed him. Got into another accident and this time it was him who died."

"No, it wasn't irony. It was suicide. He killed himself a month after the crash. Shot himself in the head."

"Well, I guess that leaves me holding the existential bag now, doesn't it?"

"No, there's no bag to hold. If I've learned anything in the nine days that I've been here, it's that there's no reason for anything," Evan said, turned around, and began to leave.

"Glad you finally fucking arrived! Welcome to the goddamn world!" Amanda shouted out after him.

At her final line, Evan swung his head over his shoulder to give her one last look. The woman in the car coming down Grant Street had her phone in her hand. She was typing in a text to say she was running late. She was unaware of the young man in the middle of the street. A toss of her phone on the passenger seat and she looked up again. It was too late to brake. The wheels of the BMW 740i she turned hard to the left. The right corner of the car missed Evan by no more than a few inches. When Amanda opened her eyes again, she saw that he had continued safely on to the other side. She watched him hurry his steps and then she watched him dash off until falling out of view.

* * *

Amanda was sitting motionless between the chains of a park swing. She was thinking how much different could death be than this life she was trapped in. How much more could she possibly take. She had her shoes off to the side and feet pushed into the sand. She had her eyes staring off and fixed on a lemonade stand some eleven years in the past. Her father was beside her scanning the neighborhood street in a rented tux. She was clenching three quarters in her hand donning a floral-print dress. In the three hours since they had been sitting there, only one cup had been sold. Placing a hand atop hers, he said, "Don't worry, pumpkin, we'll have better luck next time." She withdrew her hand from his and answered, "No, we won't. You never have any luck. It's all because of you." He stood up, kissed her on top of the head, and left. She was following him down the street wishing that she could have the day back just to scream sorry when a voice intruded upon her reverie. She was hoping it was God calling down to ask if she wanted that day back. She was hoping if not that, then maybe He was calling to ask if she wanted to leave. No such luck. No such thing.

"Hey," Evan said after closing the cover to his laptop and tucking it under an arm.

"I see we enabled Find My iPhone," Amanda replied, turning away for a second to clear the film from her eyes.

"Yeah, I lose it all the time."

"I guess I can take the listing off of eBay now," Amanda said as she reached into the front pocket of her jeans and handed Evan his phone.

"Thanks. Listen, I shouldn't have—"

"Don't. Don't do it. I'll think more of you if you don't."

Evan nodded to her advice and buried the apology he was going to bring.

"Can I sit down for a moment?" he asked.

"Sure," Amanda answered and then took a look at the sky. "They said there would be meteor showers tonight."

Evan followed her gaze and replied, "It's cloudy."

"Yeah, no shit. Once again, it'll have to come from the flick of my cigarette."

Evan watched Amanda tap the Marlboro Red and then watched as the embers fell to the ground. *Even in the state she was in, she was still so beautiful,* he thought. *It must have made everyone withdraw from telling her that the path she was on was a terrible mistake. Beauty gets away with so much. Nothing in this world has so much impunity.*

"You know here. When I'm alone. At this time of the night. It is heaven as I imagine it. No God. No people. Just me."

"That kind of eternity could get lonely."

"Couldn't be any fucking lonelier than it is here. And here, I have to share it with everyone else around. So, which do you think is worse?"

"No, if that's the way you feel, it would be better to be alone without anyone around at all. Then one wouldn't know how alone they really are."

"Exactly. I do try, though. Every day I extrapolate out a future and every tomorrow is just the same. And the same just sucks."

"Maybe you're extrapolating to the wrong point," Evan said as he turned slightly in her direction.

"No shit," Amanda replied and sucked in deep on her cigarette. And as the smoke was making its way down her lungs, she found herself once again thinking of the lemonade stand. "My father died when I was young, too."

"I'm sorry. How did he die?"

"ALS. It's a wicked fucking disease that just wastes away your belief in God in a matter of no time. I went from sitting in the front of my Catechism class just like a good little girl to one day just standing up and walking out of the room. Fuck, I'm so proud of that twelve-year-old girl."

The next question Evan had dangling on the edge of his lips. And there he let it teeter for a moment, wondering if it was the right moment to ask, wondering if she would just get up and leave. But as in all probability this would be the last time he would ever see her again, he decided to just let the question drop.

"Is that why you do it?"

"*It*, as in heroin?" she said, not even caring in the slightest that the question had been asked, not even wondering how the information had been acquired.

"Yeah."

"No, I don't do heroin because my father died. Everyone's fucking father dies at some point if they don't beat them to the punch line. I do it because my brain loves it and my body craves it. I don't blame anything or anyone. It was my decision. Um, a poor decision. But nonetheless a decision I have to live with. Although, after my little incident a few days ago, I am now clean. Again."

"I've never done any kind of drug."

"Yeah, you really don't have to tell anyone that, you know. That collared shirt from Ralph Lauren you're wearing pretty much has 'I'm Drug Free' written all over it."

"I guess it does," Evan said with a little laugh as he glanced at the monogram on his shirt and then lowered his eyes in embarrassment. And as he was waiting for her to speak again, he noticed the tattoo on her ankle. It wasn't a design, and it wasn't lettering. It was just a mark of time inked in black that told everyone whatever happened, happened at "A.M. 9:36."

"You still in school?" Amanda said so she could pull him from asking any questions about the tattoo.

"No, I graduated last week."

"And where did we go?"

"University of Chicago."

"Impressive. Major?"

"Applied mathematics. How about you?"

"Literature at Syracuse for a little while. Now just lost at sea."

"Think you'll ever go back?"

"Doubt it. But you never know. You must be heading back to Chicago soon."

"In a few days. I wanted to go to Niagara Falls."

"Never been."

"That seems kind of odd. I would think that out here in Buffalo they would have school trips there."

"They do. I was supposed to go in sixth grade, but my dad was really sick that day. After that, it's been kind of like just fuck it, you know," Amanda said.

Those last words started to make Evan realize that maybe she was lying to herself when she said the reason for doing heroin was because it was craved and loved. More likely, it seemed it was to anesthetize and escape.

"How about going with me tomorrow?"

"Fuck. Are you asking me out on a date?"

"No, no. I wasn't thinking of it in that way. I was just looking for a little company. And I thought maybe—"

"Thought maybe the misanthrope junkie needed a day with tourists and crying children."

"Sorry."

"Okay, I'm out of here. Even in my life, this is a little too bizarre," Amanda said as she pulled her toes out of the sand and slipped them into her shoes.

"Thanks again for my phone."

"Yeah, you're welcome."

Evan watched her let go of the chains and stand up. She was a few feet away when he called her back.

"Why does it suck?"

"What?" she asked, stopping and then turning around.

"Why does tomorrow always suck?"

The question took her by complete surprise. She knew exactly why tomorrow never brought what it promised. She knew she was mostly to blame. But she always thought no one ever really gave a fuck to pose the question. Just someone to care. That's all she wanted. That would have helped her to get through the next broken day.

"You know, that's the first time anyone has ever asked me that. Christ, you're the first goddamn person. What time are you going tomorrow?"

"I was thinking at dusk."

"Well, Evan from Chicago, you never know. Maybe I'll see you there."

Evan watched her backpedal a few more feet before turning a hundred and eighty degrees around. He watched her pass the fountain with four dolphins spitting water and then the red, white, and blue rocket ship. He saw her slap the head of the hippo on the merry-go-round. He saw her hit the street and then fade out of his sight like from a movie scene. He was thinking what it would be like to hold her in his arms and take away all of her pain. He was thinking that perhaps he could bring her a tomorrow when all she thought she had was today.

I'M A SLAVE TO ALWAYS FUCKING UP

A T THE SECURITY RAIL, Evan was staring out over the Falls. The sun had just lost its grip of the horizon and the inkwell spill of the night was now almost complete. He checked his watch and again promised himself that it would be the last time he took another look. Another minute or so passed and finally it set in that she wasn't going to show. It wasn't a complete defeat though he began to think. After all, she did say maybe. The rail he pushed off with both hands and decided to head back home. And then, not too far from where he originally was, he spotted her on the other side of a bench. When he walked up, he found her reading a book with her back to the lighted Falls.

"I didn't know you were here," he said, swiping a look at the "I'm A Slave To Always Fucking Up" T-shirt she was wearing.

"I knew you were."

"Oh," he answered, wondering for a moment why she didn't come up to him. "*Anna Karenina*, huh?"

"Yep. Goddamn Russians. They always take fucking forever to get to the end of one's life."

"That they do. How long have you been here?"

"About an hour or so."

"It's pretty majestic."

"It's okay. Never takes much to excite the masses," Amanda replied after flipping a page.

"I wonder what the drop is like."

Amanda briefly raised her eyes over the top of the book and then set them back onto the print. "You thinking of going over in a little barrel."

"Couldn't. I'm a little claustrophobic and a lot acrophobic."

"Those are poor excuses, Evan from Chicago. We here in Buffalo drink through all of our phobias."

"Do you want to walk around a little?"

"Oh fuck, poor Anna," Amanda said and then closed the book.

"Finished reading?"

"No and yes," Amanda answered as she got to her feet.

"I don't understand."

"Well, you asked two questions. And with regard to the second one about whether I'm done reading, that's an obvious yes. The last chapter is a waste of Russian ink."

"So, you don't want to walk around?"

"Nope," she replied. And then, without giving him notice, she began to walk off.

"Are you leaving?" Evan called out, not sure whether or not he should follow her.

"Yes, but you're coming with me."

In her reply, he left his spot and caught up with her.

"Where are we going?"

"Afraid I might take you to some drug den with all the crazed junkies?"

"No, I wasn't thinking that."

"Then just follow me."

Amanda walked them to the parking lot. There she stood with her arms folded across her chest and there she stood surveying all of the cars.

"All right, I give up. Where's the Prius?"

"The what?"

"The Prius. That's what you drive, isn't it? Not that I'm profiling or anything."

"I don't drive."

"How did you get here then?"

"Took the bus."

"And here I thought I was leaving in style. Fuck, I guess it's back on the NFTA then."

"There's one that departs from the Visitor Center in . . . in seventeen minutes," Evan said after a check of his watch.

"Did you memorize the schedule, Evan from Chicago?"

"I just looked at the one for today."

"Just today's, huh?"

"Yeah."

"Okay, ready for a pop quiz?" Amanda said as she pulled out her phone.

"On what?"

"Oh, you'll see," Amanda replied and began to do an Internet search. "Got it. So, what time does the last bus leave from here?"

"12:53 a.m."

"Wrong. I knew you didn't know."

"What time does it say?"

"12:32 a.m."

"I think you're on the Saturday schedule."

"Fuck. You're right," Amanda said after she found the header. "You just told me you only looked at today's schedule. How in the hell did you know it was 12:32 a.m. then?"

"I think I also glanced at the weekend schedules."

"Glanced at them, huh?" Amanda said with a roll of her eyes. "Okay. All right. Let's say we had cut the party here short and decided to leave on the bus before the last?"

"You mean today?"

"No, that would be too easy. Give me the second to last bus rolling out of here on Sunday?"

"Is it 10:28 p.m.?"

"You know, you're starting to make me believe that there really is a God."

"Because I know the schedule of a weekend bus."

"No, that's not the reason. I'm sure there are other freaks out there like you who have won the genetic lottery. Just a roll of the fucking dice. No big deal. The reason though, Evan from Chicago, is because if God had given me that kind of memory, He damn well would have known that l wouldn't have said, 'Is it 10:28 p.m.?' Instead, one with that kind of omniscience would understand that out of my mouth would have come, 'It's ten fucking twenty-eight. What's the goddamn big deal? Christ, is this world full of fucking simpletons.' "

"We should probably start heading to the bus station, huh?"

"Yep, we probably should," Amanda replied.

* * *

They were ten or so minutes into the ride. Not a word had yet passed between either of them, even though both had questions to ask. Evan was sitting window-side, staring out at nothing in particular. He was wishing he had brought along a notebook so he could write down every question he had in his head. This way, it would be so much easier to begin. He would hand her the notebook along with a pen so she could pick and choose which ones she was comfortable answering. Question number one would be a benign and simple introduction. Number one would be: "What's your middle name?" The second would be: "Did you like high school?" And number three would read: "Do you have any brothers or sisters?" The fourth question though was the one that made him delete everything he had typed into his mind and realize he had to start again. The fourth one was where he asked: "Could you ever see yourself dating someone like me?"

Amanda had her feet up on the cloth seat and her arms wrapped around her knees. She had her blue-tinted aviator sunglasses over her eyes. This to her was always akin to making sure only the cover of the book was being read and not what was on the pages inside. Hands between her legs, she was using her thumb to dig into her fingers. This to her was always the way she kept from speaking what she knew shouldn't be said. On her tongue, she had the words: *Why in the hell are you even wasting your time after finding out your father died to save a heroin addict?* On her tongue, she had the question: *Why travel this far when in the end, the past doesn't really fucking matter anyway?* On her tongue, she wanted to pose: *If you're going to forgive all that, then why in the hell haven't you kissed me yet?* Instead, after looking at his sweet face in the reflection of the bus window, she softened and asked: "Is the reason you don't drive because of your father?"

"I guess so," Evan answered with a quick look in her direction.

"You ride in cars though, right?"

"When I have to. It just makes me really anxious, so I prefer not to."

"And busses, obviously."

"Yeah, I'm okay with them for some reason. Probably because they're a lot larger, I'm assuming. I don't know."

"Well, Evan from Chicago, wouldn't ya know, we're birds of a feather. I don't drive either."

"Really?"

"Yep."

"Why not?"

"Because my mother was a bitch and told me there was no way in hell she was going to let me use her car until after I graduated high school. Then, after I went off to Syracuse, there was no real reason to have one except to come home. And since I sure in the fuck didn't want to do that, I used it as the reason why I never visited her for a year and a half. In the end, it seemed to work out in my favor."

"She probably didn't want you to drive because of the accident."

"Yeah, I'm sure that probably was the reason. The problem was that she never mentioned it to me. I needed some kid to come all the way from Chicago six years later and let me in on the family secret."

"Have you gone back since you left college?"

"A few times. To pick up stuff, you know. But it's so goddamn awkward, and all we do is fight. It's like seeing an ex-boyfriend and him not getting it in his head that we've broken up for good."

"Oh, I was going to ask you this. Do you have any brothers or sisters?"

"Only child just like you."

"How did you know that?"

"I didn't until now, but I had a feeling. I always seem to know when someone doesn't have any siblings. The conversations are just so different. Not a lot of bullshit is said when you talk to them. And they always seem to have a little more gravitas than everyone else."

"Did you ever wish you weren't?"

"An only child?"

"Yeah."

"When my dad was alive, I was glad I was the only one so I didn't have to share him with anyone else. After he died though, yeah I wished I wasn't. I wished that I had about ten other brothers and sisters so all that loss and bullshit could have been divided up and shared equally. How about you?"

"I guess there were times when I wanted an older brother. Someone who could show me how to hit a baseball or someone who could stick up for me when I was getting picked on at school. A surrogate for my father, you know. That would have been nice, I suppose. But most of the time, I didn't mind being alone. I kept myself busy."

"Doing what?"

"I don't know. You have to give me an age."

"Let's say twelve. What did the Midwest Ivy League scholar do when he was twelve?"

"Probably nothing different from any other twelve-year-old."

"I find that hard to believe, Evan from Chicago. You're a University of Chicago mathematics graduate. I can't believe any of you grew up normal. Your synapses are probably so busy exchanging numbers back and forth that I'm assuming there's not an open line left to call up the outside world."

"It wasn't like I was sitting in my room doing math equations when I was that age."

"Then what were you doing?"

"The usual things, I guess. Reading, taking bike rides, working with the chemistry set I got for that Christmas, playing video chess a lot. You know. Just hanging out."

"Obviously, you weren't able to fit in the debate club because that last statement did nothing to support your argument of a normal twelve-year-old existence."

"Okay, fine. I didn't have a lot of friends. Actually, to tell you the truth, I didn't even have anyone I could call my best friend. I was terrible at sports. I was shy. And most of the time I spent wishing the next grade would come and I would somehow change."

"See, wasn't that therapeutic?"

"No, not really. How about you? What were you like at twelve?"

"Well, Evan, twelve was a shit year for Amanda Smith. She spent most of her time outside of school inside of a hospital. No chemistry set, bike rides, or video chess for her."

"Your dad?"

"Yep."

"I'm sorry. That must have been terrible to go through."

"Yeah, it did suck actually. But I'm sure it sucked more so for my dad so who would I be to bitch about it."

"Were you there when he passed?"

"Right beside him at nine thirty-six in the morning. Saw him gasp that last breath and then for some reason checked my Hello Kitty watch. That's pretty bizarre that I would do that, huh?"

"I don't know. Is there any reaction that can be considered normal after you just lost the most important thing in your life?"

"Just fucking typical."

"What? Did I say something wrong?"

"No, you didn't say anything wrong. I was just thinking that if I had you as a friend when I was growing up, I just might have had a chance."

It was the word "friend" that turned him away from the conversation and back to the window where he had originally started. It was that word that made him realize he was just a guest in her world and nothing more. All those parts of her life she was telling him were only because she was being asked, and not because she felt he was the only one who would understand.

Evan's sudden reticence Amanda took as an intermission and nothing else. She was actually glad that silence had intervened for a moment as it gave her time to go back over the transcript of what had been said. *All these goddamn questions he keeps asking. And why in the hell am I even answering all these doors he keeps knocking at when in a few days he'll return to where he came. And maybe, that's why in the end it won't matter anyway. So, you have a good look at as many of my rooms as you fucking wish, Evan from Chicago. They're all yours to walk around in. In a few days, we'll forget like we've never met.*

The bus slowed to a stop. Evan gave her a glance and hoped she would be looking back. However, she was staring ahead like he wasn't even sitting next to her. Her seeming indifference was the final confirmation that he could have been just anybody. Though he barely knew her and had no reason to want her, oddly he felt a snap inside that felt like the break of a heartstring.

A close of the doors and time forward again. Amanda hurried a look over her shoulder to try and get a read of the sign to see where they were at.

"Did you get what stop that was?" she asked.

"Yeah. Black Rock Riverside. Why, did you want to get off?"

"No, we're going to the end of the line. Fuck though, that went fast, didn't it? Jesus, it seems like we just got on this bus."

"We left at seven after nine. So, twenty-eight minutes."

"Christ, that figures, ever since I turned twelve everything around me feels like it's been moving at light speed. My father got sick and then he was dead. I was graduating high school and then I was dropping out of college. I was moving into The Nucleus and then I was with John. I became a heroin addict and now two years later, I'm strangely here with you. Fuck, at this pace, I'll be dead before I turn twenty-three."

"I feel just the opposite. It seems like it's taken me a lifetime to arrive here. I feel like I've already lived a hundred years."

"I'd trade lives with you, but I sure in the fuck don't want a hundred years of living behind me either."

"You don't want to get old?"

"God, no. I barely want to be young."

Amanda's last statement was an end to their conversation on the bus as both faded away into thought. Twenty minutes later, they pulled into the Buffalo Transportation Center. Another segment of time and they were walking out on the streets. One point three miles then erased, and Amanda stopped their forward progress in front of a Romanesque and Renaissance structure built of deep red Medina limestone. Three arched entrances faced them. On the left, the tallest of the steeples reached perhaps five stories high. On the right, the second steeple maybe just three. Where stained glass windows must have been, sadly now only wooden boards filled the openings. Amanda nodded over to it to let him know that they had arrived. It was a rhetorical gesture though as from the one lone window that had not been boarded up, multicolored lasers were sweeping about inside and a healthy bass beat was spilling out onto Main Street.

"It's a church," Evan said.

"Not anymore. All those sad faces praying for an afterlife have been replaced by those worshipping the very moment they live in."

"Do we enter here?"

"No, the entrance is on the side. Come on."

As they walked on, Amanda had her fingers spread out so that they were brushing across the sandstone blocks. Suddenly, she stopped and reached out to take Evan's wrist. His hand she placed on one of those blocks and hers she placed right on top.

"What are we doing?" Evan asked.

"Listening with our hands. I found a weak spot."

"I don't know what you mean."

"Can't you feel that?"

"The vibration?"

"Yeah, the vibration. Whenever I come here, I search for a weak spot. And since you were mentioning it, I wanted to show you what I think it must feel like to be old. I think it's just like the walls of this building. You're neglected and crumbling on the outside. But on the inside, you still have a heart that beats wild. It must just make you so fucking crazy that you want to scream. And that would just suck, wouldn't it now?"

"And so, what's the analog for barely wanting to be young?"

"Like being in a new house with nothing but old furniture inside."

They came to the entrance. The line was a queue of three. As the bouncer was talking to those who had come before them, Evan took a moment to stare at him. A good guess would have put him at six foot five. Another would have placed him in his mid-thirties, though with that boyish face he could have easily passed for twenty-five. His head was razored to the skin, and through the lobes of his ears, 8-gauge obsidian stone saddle plugs were set in. He had on combat boots perfectly laced to their final eyelets. He had on a Mickey Mouse tee, and over that a black leather vest that barely fit across his barreled chest. On one of the cannons he had for arms, a Celtic cross had been tattooed. And through the loops of his jeans, a black leather pyramid-studded belt.

"Amanda," the bouncer said after the group had gone in. He said after taking a quick look at Evan and filling up his face with a smile because it wasn't John beside her.

"James," she replied.

"You need two cups?"

"Yeah, we're drinking. How much tonight?" she asked while starting to reach into the front pocket of her jeans.

"Put it away. They're on me."

"Thank you."

To the wooden barstool next to him, the bouncer reached over, and from a stack three feet high handed her two red Solo cups.

"You out here all night?" Amanda then asked after she handed Evan one of the cups.

"Only another hour. Brenden's taking watch then. Gotta get home to the twins."

"Tell Sam I said hi."

"Will do. You should call her. She'd love to hear from ya."

"Yeah," she said as the bouncer opened the door.

Evan entered first, and just as she started to go through, the bouncer had a few more words for her.

"Hey."

"What?"

"You're looking good."

She understood he meant it not as a compliment on how she looked. She knew it was a euphemism for: "Glad to see that you're not fucking wasted again." A half-smile was her reply because anything larger than that would have been a lie. Anything larger than that would have locked her into next time showing up clean.

Inside, the introduction was a rectangular anteroom that was thirty feet wide and extended twenty feet forward. Once upon a time, it acted as a soundproof box for crying babies who couldn't keep quiet during Mass. Once upon a time, it was a repository for missalettes and corkboards with pinned announcements of the newly arrived and the recently departed. Back then and long ago, it had two life-size statues in each corner, one of the Mother Mary cradling her infant Son and the other some friend of hers who was now a saint. Once the walls were of wood paneling and the lighting high above incandescent bulbs. Now, the lights were purple LEDs, and the wood paneling replaced with drywall covered in fluorescent glow light paint. Now, in lieu of the statues, were half kegs of craft IPAs and Belgium ales. And, like the "All Souls Deuteronomy," the rules of The Nucleus were handwritten on a scroll. Fifteen feet long and hanging from the back wall, they were there for all to read and obey.

Everyone is Welcome

Respect the rights and liberties of self-expression

Assume civic responsibility

Creative collaboration and cooperation is expected

Discover, exercise, and rely on your inner resources

Remember to Participate

Leave no trace

Gifting is unconditional

No commercial sponsorships, transactions, or advertising

Immediacy is the Most Important of All of These

Head titled up, Evan stood reading the list. Amanda removed the cup from his hand and went over to one of the kegs. A moment later, she returned with two full cups and handed him one.

"Thanks," Evan said and then watched her walk to one of the walls, and from a metal pail, pick up a stick of fuchsia-colored chalk. In between all of the other musings, she wrote in a quote that had been swirling around in her mind for the last few days.

In my beginning is my end - T. S. Eliot

Evan broke from where he was standing and walked over to her.

"I've never read anything by Eliot."

"Well, now you have," she answered, holding the piece of chalk for him to take and put down some ephemeral legacy of his own.

"I don't think I have anything important to say," he said while looking at all of the other writings adorning the wall.

"Yeah, same thought for me. That's why I stole the line. Go ahead. No points deducted for plagiarism."

"Okay," Evan said.

> *The first principle is that you must not fool yourself,*
> *and you are the easiest person to fool.*
> *- Richard Feynman*

"All right, I'm thinking even a good Google search wouldn't know who the fuck Richard Feynman is," Amanda said after he had finished and returned to her side.

"No, it would come up. He won a share of the Noble Prize in physics. Why? You don't like it?"

"Just messing with ya. It's good. Real good. You ready to go in?"

"Sure."

Amanda led the way, pushing through one of the two wooden doors. Evan hadn't taken more than a few steps when he stopped in wonderment. The stroboscopic lights were pulsing their xenon flash lamps at 200 microseconds. Brilliant beams like Jedi lightsabers were crisscrossing the air. North to south, east to west, the first floor was a ballroom for society's outcasts, a church for its misfits. Neon signs of love and peace. Graffiti-covered walls in outcries against war and hate. A girl in leather, her man in a dress. Skateboarders tricking on the halfpipe. Fire jugglers spinning their pois. Kids with lighted hula hoops twisting to and fro. A pair of queens wearing heart and diamond dresses, like only true trans soul rebels could. A kid on stilts walking about. Another in the middle of it all playing violin. It was a furlough from the chains of money and fame. It was a respite from the cease and surrender.

It was a night in the lighted garden of whatever you ever wanted to be.

The last four beats of the song played, and then the house lights came on. Evan thought it was the end of the night. Amanda understood it was just a DJ's reprieve for everyone to regroup and reassemble. A flick of a switch, a bass drop, and everything electric once more. Ten seconds in and the digitized voice of a Danish girl sent everyone back into a frenzy.

"What do you think?" Amanda shouted to him.

"It's mesmerizing. I've never seen anything like it."

"Yeah, that was the point," she replied, a bit superciliously, but inside a little pleased that she was bringing something new to him.

"What is it?"

"Friday Night Flow Jam. A lot of performers and artists come here to either practice their chops or skillshare. Everyone else, just here to step away for a few hours from the court."

"The court of what?" Evan questioned.

"The court of society. Outside of here, we are all judged. Inside, no one is on trial."

"It doesn't seem like your type of music," Evan said.

"It's not. But I do like the electricity. It makes me feel alive. Something I don't get outside of here."

Just after she finished speaking, one of the fire jugglers broke from his routine and started to walk over. When he got close enough, Evan was able to get a good look at the sleeve and neck tattoos, along with the silver nose ring and the black beret he wore. He gave Evan a glance and then Amanda a big hug.

"How's it going, Amanda?" he asked after breaking from the

embrace.

"Good days. Bad days. Just like the rest of the world, trying to survive, you know."

"Who'd ya bring?"

"Well, Medic, you are in for a real treat. This is Evan from Chicago. I've brought him here to see what the rest of the world has been doing while he's been renumbering the universe."

"Cool," he said to Amanda, then turned to Evan. "Evan from Chicago, welcome to The Nucleus."

Evan held out his hand to have shaken. The fire juggler went right past it and gave him a crushing hug.

"It's just Evan," Evan said across his ear.

"You gonna stay?" Medic asked of Amanda.

"For a little bit."

"Cool. Listen, I gotta get ready for a performance we're putting on in about fifteen minutes."

"All right. We'll stay to check it out."

"Okay, I'm outta here. Amanda, good seeing ya again. Evan from Chicago, glad you came."

"Me too," Evan replied, waiting for another hug. This time though, Medic held out a fist on which the letters B-E-A-S-T were tattooed on the knuckles. Evan gave it a bump and Amanda watched Medic fold into the crowd before turning to Evan.

"You want a tour?"

"Yeah, sure," Evan answered.

"Good, then follow me."

Amanda led the way. Evan followed behind still in awe. She was three-quarters up a ladder to the second floor when she stopped and turned her head back.

"You coming?"

"Yeah, I was just holding the ladder. I wanted to make sure you got up."

Evan did a slow and careful climb to the top. When he finally arrived, she took his hand for the final step. He wished he had another four or five rungs left because he didn't want to let go.

"So, this is where choir practice is held," Amanda said as she nodded toward the back of the area they were in.

"You mean where bands practice, right?" Evan said as he looked at the setup of a seven-piece drum kit, two Marshall stacks on each side of it, a microphone stand, and a twenty-four channel mixer.

"Sorry, I'll be more literal during the tour," Amanda said and then pointed off to her right. "Over there are seven of the glass-stained windows that for some fucking reason were removed. They're fucking phenomenal. My favorite is the one of Mary at the Crucifixion. The colors are just so striking."

"You mind if I have a look at it?"

"Be my guest, Evan from Chicago. That's why we started the GoFundMe page that was able to pay for them."

Evan walked over to it while Amanda took only half of his steps. Looking it over, it became obvious it wasn't the colors that she adored. More likely, he thought, it was the crushing sorrow of it all.

"You believe in God?" Evan asked after a quick turn of his head.

"While my father was sick, I used to beg to Him every day."

"And now?"

"Now? No, not now. Now we don't speak. Now I've replaced Him with other things that can get me to heaven faster. You done here?"

"Yeah, I'm done."

"Up above is the balcony where you can see the pipe organ."

"Does it still work?"

"Sporadically. I've heard them get it going a few times."

"I don't understand this floor. It couldn't have been here when this place used to be a church. Who put it in?"

"Some developer. It was supposed to be converted to lofts, but he lost funding a quarter way through and that's when we moved in. Sucked for him. But I think we made better use of it than a bunch of gentrifying fucks ever could. You want to see where I used to live?"

"Sure."

Amanda moved the both of them on, underneath the pipe organ and then down a path that narrowed into a long corridor. As he followed, he was glancing into the rooms on both sides of him. Six or seven of them he passed before realizing there was an obvious omission.

"None of these rooms have doors," he stated.

"Yeah, I love that about this place. All of the other places I lived had doors, and most of the time I ended up locking myself behind them," Amanda said as she stopped at the last room on the left and did a quick check inside. After finding it unoccupied, she entered and was flooded with thoughts of what could have been if she had just stayed still and never left.

Evan stood at the threshold and swept his eyes about an area he figured was no larger than the dorm room he shared with Ashok. To his right, a bunk bed of reclaimed pallet wood occupied the space. Directly across, a long rectangular window started from the floor and ran thirteen feet before falling just short of the ceiling. On his left, a white and black tapestry decorated the brick wall. The design was simple, vertical and horizontal lines built up the gallows from where hung a stick figure replete with all of its body parts. Underneath, the word hadn't been completed, but it was so, so obvious. Underneath, only three letters had been filled in: _ M _ N D _. He stayed preoccupied with it a little too long. He stayed wondering what makes someone hang themselves in a child's game.

"Curious as to why it's still there?" she said.

"Yeah," he answered politely, figuring it was just best to let the artist drive the conversation while he resolved himself to accept any explanation that was to be given.

"Nucleus rules."

"I don't understand what that means."

"Everyone has to leave a piece of themselves behind before they move out. Sign it, and no one touches it. That's why it's still hanging here."

"Who owns this place now?" he asked.

"Everyone, basically. You never heard of co-op living?"

"No, not really."

"Jesus, you are the sheltered one."

"What does it cost to live here?"

"I don't know what they pay now, but when I was here, it was about three hundred a month."

"Did you live here long?"

"About a year."

"Why did you leave?"

"Because I met John."

"Mailbox John?"

"Yeah, Mailbox John. At first, he thought it was cool. Then, after he sucked me into his vortex, he told me he didn't approve of me sharing a space with mostly other guys. So, me being the codependent fuck that I am, I left and moved in with him."

Evan departed from Amanda for a moment and walked over to the window. The Buffalo skyline was in view, its gilded lights giving it a certain warmth and charm he never would have imagined without having seen it from this height. To his lips, he lifted the plastic cup in his hands and took an uncharacteristically long drink. Though he wasn't drunk, the alcohol was just enough for him to consider moving here so that he could be nearer to her.

"It can't be that captivating. It's only Buffalo, you know."

"Sorry, I was drifting off," he said, turning around and leaning his back against the wall.

"Where did you get that watch?" Amanda asked as she caught the cracked face of it when he moved the cup to his lips, and it slipped out from underneath a sleeve.

"It was my dad's. My mother gave it to me when I turned ten."

After he answered, it occurred to her that he never even glanced at it like anyone else would have. And then it occurred to her that most likely it was the one his father was wearing when he was hit by the truck.

"What did he do for a living?"

"Taught mathematics at a high school. My mom said he was brilliant. She said he had a lot of offers when he graduated with his doctorate, but I guess he just decided to teach high school kids instead."

"Just taught high school, huh? That's a pretty big fucking deal if you think about it. I mean who would possibly want to put up with all of the teenage assholes of the world. Most of whom who could really give a shit about anything, much less never-ending math equations. Fuck, it sounds to me like he decided to go noble instead of selling out to the corporate pricks."

"No, I know. I didn't phrase that the way I probably should have."

"Do you remember anything about him?"

"Only from the pictures and videos my mother had of him. When I was younger, I used to go through them all of the time. But it's really weird when you don't remember them. It's like downloading memories from someone else's family. You don't feel a part of any of it. You're just a passive observer. How about you? What do you remember about your father?"

"Too fucking much. That's what I remember. And a lot of times after I bring them up for recall, I wish I was amnesic. Memory can really suck." Amanda turned her head to the side, exhaled a deep breath to keep the tears from coming, and then stood up from the bed when she noticed the music had stopped. "Come on. We should go. They're going to be starting soon."

Amanda and Evan took the ladder back down, where they seated themselves in an imperfect circle with all the others who had come to watch. The house lights went to black, and after a moment of silence, the synthesizer was punching out the beats like quick jabs from a prizefighter. Five on the floor, the jugglers began by tilting their heads as far back as they could, and from their mouths, jetting streams of fire into the air. Now lit, they started to spin their multi-wick fire poi staffs until triple rings of fire appeared to be suspended three feet off of the ground.

During the performance, Amanda kept casting intermittent glances over to Evan. She was close enough to see the show in his eyes. To her, he looked no older than sixteen. To her, in another lifetime and in another world, she thought she could easily see her hand interlocked within his and her head resting upon his shoulder. They would go home together, and she would wake up with his arms around her. It only took another thought for her to realize that what she was imagining was another fucking ephemeral tease. So, she quickly put her mind back on what she dreamed best, a funeral pyre with her the guest of honor.

"Wow, that was incredible," Evan said as the performance had come to an end.

"It is pretty cool, isn't it? Medic's the fucking best. I love watching him perform," she replied, even though she had caught only half of the act as her eyes had spent the other time watching him.

"Has he been doing it long?" Evan asked.

"For as long as I've known him."

"You miss this place, huh?"

Amanda was nodding her head to the past when the house lights switched on to make friends of everyone who had come. By the time the keyboard had delivered the fourth stanza, the rest of the congregation had already hit the floor. The bass line soon followed, and the introduction may have seemed a bit stretched, but it was an intentional light of a long wick before the fireworks were to begin. This one may have always gotten played, but no one gets tired when the words are worth more now than they were yesterday. For those old enough to remember, the guitar riff to come may have been more reminiscent of a new order. But then again, who in the hell cares when the only reason you are here is to forget what came before.

That's how it starts
We go back to your house
We check the charts
And start to figure it out

"Let's go," Amanda said as she took hold of his hand for the second time in the night and motioned for him to follow.

"Are we leaving?" he asked.

"From where we are standing, yes. But if you're referring to The Nucleus. Then that would be a no."

With Evan in tow, Amanda wended her way through the crowd until she found a space with just enough room for the two of them to comfortably fit. He stood still and watched as she began into a slow sway that immediately locked into resonance with the heartbeat of the song. It wasn't that she seemed out of place or that any of her movements were maladroit. On the contrary, she looked more beautiful and more alive than he had seen her at any other time. It was just that he was a little shocked since she didn't seem like the type who would join in with the masses.

"What?" she shouted over to him. He said nothing, but she knew what he was thinking. "Don't be so surprised, Evan from Chicago. Addicts can dance too."

"It's not that," he lied, but it didn't matter anyway as the music was too loud for the voice he had replied with.

> *And so it starts*
> *You switch the engine on*
> *We set the controls for the heart of the sun*
> *One of the ways we show our age*

Evan left Amanda for a moment and panned about. It reminded him of a five-hundred planet solar system. Everyone was twisting and jumping on their own axis all the while their hearts and souls were revolving around the song. For those who had brought along glow sticks, they had since been broken and looped around their necks and wrists. The disco ball left no one untouched with its tiny orbs of cool white, and the fog machines were leaving everyone knee-deep in rolling clouds. He returned to her a look and began to wonder how many boys had seen her dance like this, and how many had seen her smile like this. Both thoughts made him more jealous than the image of any one of them watching her undress. This was a privilege, this was the ultimate backstage pass.

Finally, he tried to fall into the beat by first rocking back and forth. But with his body not following suit, he was just a metronome head with skinny legs and arms. Amanda now had her eyes closed, and that gave him the opportunity to read the lyrics coming off of her lips. She didn't seem to miss a single one. She seemed to have studied hard for this test. And God how he wished he knew a song like that because when she sang "Though when we're running out of the drugs and the conversation's winding away, I wouldn't trade one stupid decision for another five years of life," he realized those words must have made so much sense to her life.

Verse by verse the cathedral had almost been built, and the parishioners now had their tambourine hands raised high into the air. In unison, they were bouncing up and down, and the floorboards beneath their feet were shaking in resonance. It was a night-inning rally into the night. It was an end-of-the-world party. Evan tried to get Amanda's attention. He took one step forward. He shouted her name. However, it soon became apparent that it was all in vain as she had already left her body and cleared orbit. She was gone, and he hoped the song would never end so she could keep drifting off to find whatever needed to be found.

> *If I could see all my friends tonight*
> *If I could see all my friends tonight*
> *If I could see all my friends tonight*
> *If I could see all my friends tonight*

When the song ended, Amanda motioned with a wave of her hand for Evan to follow her. Through the crowd she wedged a path until the two of them were out the exit door. A light mist was now falling, and their ears were still ringing with a white-noise memory of what had just been pumped into their heads. She closed her eyes and titled her face up to get in the way of the rain. The water on her skin made her look younger and inviolate. It made her lashes blacker and her lips redder. It made her look like she was new and whole again.

"God, I love the fucking rain," she said with a few shakes of her head. "It always feels like it's washing everything away and giving me another chance to change."

"To change what?"

"My life."

"You can change it without the rain, you know."

"Yeah, I'm sure there are people who can. I'm not one of them, though. For some reason, I always need a cue."

"Do you want to go home now?"

"No, I just want to take a walk."

"Where to?"

"You always need a reason for your next step?"

"I . . . I was just wondering."

"Well, let me tell you, Evan from Chicago, always mapping out a future murders serendipity. And we need serendipity to misbelieve that there's a reason for everything."

Amanda started walking them off. Halfway down the block, a voice called out that turned both of them around.

"Amanda!" Medic yelled as he stood just outside the entrance to The Nucleus. The rain was falling harder now, and none of them seemed to care. All traveled equidistance from where they stood.

"Going for a smoke or heading out?" Medic asked.

"No, I think we're leaving. You were great. It was a really cool show."

"Thanks for coming."

"Yeah, I'll see ya around."

"You're not going to Skate Plaza tomorrow?"

"For what?"

"Oh hell, you don't know, do ya?"

"Know what?"

"We're having a midnight memorial for Tommy. He OD'd two days ago."

Amanda stood there dazed for a moment, lifting her eyes up over Medic and landing them somewhere off in the distance. When she felt Evan's hand fall upon her shoulder, she tore it off like it was from an obtruder and then started to slowly backpedal. She was a few feet away from the destruction when she spun around and started into a full sprint. Medic gave a nod to Evan for him to follow her. Evan nodded back and gave chase. A block down he lost sight of her. Hands on his hips at the corner of Summer and Linwood, he searched about before finally finding her sitting against the trunk of a maple tree. He walked the remaining distance and crouched before her.

"What can I do for you?"

"Not a goddamn thing. Leave me the fuck alone," she answered and put her face back to her knees.

"No. I'm not going to do that."

"Well, find a way, will ya."

Evan sat across from her. He grabbed a stray leaf and started twirling it by the stem. His head he had down and his eyes he had staring at the grass. He knew better than to leave, and he knew better than to speak. She was strong, and he knew she just needed a few minutes to extricate herself from the wreck. Finally, she untangled herself and spoke.

"Fuck, every time. Every goddamn time I let myself start to enjoy a day, something comes into my life to tap me on the shoulder to say you know better than that," Amanda said, more to herself than to Evan.

"How did you know him?"

"From The Nucleus. He was like a brother to me when I lived there. Man, we had a lot of great times together. I just can't believe he's dead."

"I'm so sorry, Amanda. I really am."

"That's three now this year. Three people I've loved and three people who've died. Why am I the lucky one? Who the fuck wants to live through something like that? Why in the hell is breathing involuntary?"

She shifted her body to the side to take out a neon purple lighter and a pack of smokes from the front pocket of her jeans. The lighter that wouldn't hold a flame she tossed to the street, and the cigarette between her lips she wrapped a palm around and crushed. At the futility of life and the privation of a simple delight, she coughed out a laugh. A shift of her eyes to nowhere. A catatonic stare and now she had disappeared. Evan could barely see her now. Her rain-soaked hair was tendrilous and matted to her face. He took his hand and combed half of it behind an ear. It was a touch that made her feel once again. It was a gesture that finally made her capitulate. She put her arms around him and settled her head onto a shoulder of his. He held her there, hoping he could take on board at least some of her suffering.

After a few moments, he eased her to her feet, and they both stood up as if they had just risen from the sea. The rain had passed, and now only droplets from the canopy of leaves above were falling on them. She folded her arms across her chest to stave off the cold chill that had suddenly settled in. The arms to the University of Chicago hoodie he had around his waist he untied and presented her with.

"It's a little wet, but it's something."

"Thanks," she said and slipped it over her head. Even though it had soaked up a bit of water, it still felt good to be covered in. She wanted to add that she wasn't good for anyone, and if not that, she wanted to say that she would only hurt him. In the end, she settled on telling him that she wanted to walk home alone.

"Okay," he answered. "As long as you're going to be all right."

"I'll be fine. I seem to have this guardian angel whom I just can't seem to fucking shake."

"Maybe there's a reason for that."

"I doubt it," she replied and then scuffed the ground with the tip of her shoe. "Listen, I'm gonna get going."

Evan nodded and watched her as she began to walk off. She was a few houses away when she stopped and turned around.

"Hey."

"Yeah," he answered.

"You know where Skate Plaza is?"

"No, but I can find it."

"Can you meet me there tomorrow at midnight?"

"Yeah, I can do that."

ALL OF THIS SHIT 4 WHAT?

E VAN STOOD WITH A LIGHTED CANDLE held tight in the clutches of his hands. He was on the fringe of a semicircle four deep with kids not too much older than his own age, all who had candles of their own to hold. With them, he was watching a group of skateboarders in the middle of Skate Plaza doing their tricks on the ramps and stair handrails. They were all dressed up in black. They were all expressionless as if tonight they had put on masks of themselves so that they couldn't be seen laughing or crying. In his mind, he was wondering if there really was a place we go after this. In his head, he was thinking about what it would be like to have your body and mind want something so bad that you would die for it.

Amanda tapped the shoulder of the girl to the left of Evan and with her eyes, asked that she slide a few steps to the side. Evan didn't need to turn. He could smell the scent of her soap, and he could smell the scent of alcohol on her breath. From a back pocket, he pulled out a candle, lit it from his, and then held it out for her to take.

"Been here long?" she asked, her eyes darting from one skateboarder to the next.

"About a half hour."

"Thanks for showing up."

"Yeah, no problem. You okay?" he questioned, finally looking over to her and noticing she was wearing the University of Chicago hoodie he had given her the night before.

"No, I'm a fucking wreck to tell you the truth," she said and then pulled out a 200 ml bottle of Skol vodka lifted from a liquor store just fifteen minutes before. When she brought it to her lips, he noticed it was already half empty.

"You think you should be drinking?"

"More than I think I should be shooting heroin."

Evan found the reply logical and said nothing more. Amanda took another swig just to make her point. A few minutes passed between them before the conservation began again.

"He had a lot of friends, huh?" Evan said after wandering his eyes about and guessing that there were probably a hundred or so people in attendance.

"Yeah, everyone in our community loved him," she answered.

"How old was he?"

"Twenty. For me, way past life expectancy. For him, though, just starting out. It's odd now that I think about it. I never thought of him as someone who would even consider using. For the year that I lived in the room with him, he just smoked a lot of weed and read a lot of books. I wasn't shooting yet, but there were a lot of people around us who were, especially when we had events or parties. I made fucking sure though that everyone knew he was off-limits."

"How'd he get hooked then?"

"I don't know. It was definitely after I left. Can't really blame him, though. It was probably like being at an amusement park and watching as all your friends keep hopping on the rollercoaster. Eventually, you're not going to remain standing there at the end of the ride. Eventually, you're going to say to yourself I want to get in and give this thing a try. It can't be that bad because they keep getting on it again and again."

"Was he from Buffalo?"

"No, Pittsburgh. He moved out here to live with his grandparents when he was sixteen. Right after his mom and dad were killed by a drunk driver."

"That really sucks."

"Yeah, it does really suck."

The skateboarders started to leave and everyone in the circle began to move closer. After a few minutes, all that was left in the middle of Skate Plaza was a lone skateboard, and standing right beside it, a young girl whom Evan guessed to be a few years younger than him. One by one, someone broke from the circle and stepped before the girl. Her lips she aimed at the candle, closed her eyes, and then blew out the flame. Amanda went before Evan. The girl smiled when she saw her face. Amanda watched the flame of her candle bend and stretch before succumbing to the weight of the girl's breath. From the pocket of the hoodie, she unearthed a silver skateboard charm. It was recognized immediately. It was the one Tommy had worn on a chain around his neck since he was eight. It was the one he had given to Amanda the night she had moved out of The Nucleus. In the girl's palm she placed it and folded her fingers over it. A kiss on the cheek, a hug, and then Amanda walked off.

Evan stepped before the girl. Up close, he was now able to get a better look. And if not for the sleeve tattoo on her left arm, she was an exact copy of a girl he once knew from his freshman year at university. She had straight cinnamon-colored hair that lay flat just beyond her chest. She had on a knee-length blue and white patterned skirt. She had moss green eyes and she still had her freckles from childhood. The candle he held up higher and waited for her to snuff it out in one deep breath. She was tired though and she was angry now. She reached out and took the life of the flame with her palm. Her hand was shaking, but her face was expressionless. Slowly, Evan lowered the candle from her grip. *One death and the living all fall,* he thought.

Through the crowd, Evan wandered around searching for Amanda. He found her five minutes later. He found her standing by Medic and a group of friends. He watched embraces given and tears bled. He then watched as something seemed to take her attention away. From the group she broke and began to walk off. That walk quickly turned into a full-out sprint. He thought she was fleeing until he watched her give some guy in his mid-thirties a hard shove in the back. The guy fell over like a domino, and when he turned around, she kicked him in the stomach.

"What the fuck, Amanda?" the guy said through the hands he had moved from his stomach to his face as he saw her foot getting ready to strike again.

"You got a lot of goddamn balls showing up here, Ryan."

"What are you talking about?"

"You sold it to him, didn't you?"

"No, I didn't sell it to him."

"You're a fucking liar! Just like all the other dope dealers!" she screamed down to him.

"Can you please lower your voice? There are a few cops around."

"Good. Because after I get done with you, I'm going to grab one of 'em and tell him to arrest your fucking ass."

"I'm telling you. I didn't sell it to him, Amanda. The last time I saw Tommy was a few months ago."

"Then who did?"

"May I get up?"

Amanda stepped back and he took that for a yes.

"Jesus, that fucking hurt, Amanda. Why the hell did you have to kick me?"

"Because you're a dope dealer and a goddamn murderer. How's that for a motive? Now tell me who the fuck sold it to him."

"I have no idea. There are twenty dealers I could name off the top of my head who could have sold it to him. You know that. Everyone's dealing it. Hell, why are you blaming me?"

"Cause he always went to you."

"Yeah, you're right. He always did come to me. That was until I cut him off."

"And why the fuck would you cut him off? You'd sell it to your own mother."

"Oh, Jesus Christ, Amanda, did you have to say that. My mother is dead."

"So what."

"All right, so what. But if we could off get the subject of my dead mother for a moment, I'll tell you the reason why."

"Go ahead."

"The reason I wouldn't sell to him is because he was already two hundred into me. I told him I wasn't going to front him any more until he cleared the tab."

"Bullshit."

"Amanda, I'm telling you the truth. I liked the kid a lot. And besides, I try all the shit that comes through me. It wouldn't be good for business if I started killing off all my clients."

"You are such an asshole."

"Yes, I am such an asshole. But I'm one of the benevolent ones."

"I swear, if I find out it was you, I'm going to set you on fucking fire."

"I know you would, Amanda. I know you would."

The commotion brought Medic and the group of friends beside Amanda. A few steps later it also brought Evan.

"You all right?" Medic asked.

"Yeah, I'm fine," Amanda replied.

"Are you done with me?" the dealer asked, afterward giving a check to the semicircle of faces that had gathered.

"Yeah, get the fuck out of here."

Given permission, the dealer left. Amanda drew in a deep breath to settle down and then raked a hand through her hair to set back the long strands that had fallen all about her face.

"You guys need a ride?" Medic asked her.

"No, we're fine," Amanda replied.

"Okay. If you need someone to talk to, just stop by anytime," he said to Amanda.

"Yeah, thanks."

Amanda gave Medic a hug and a short wave to the others. She started walking with Evan in no particular direction when after exiting Skate Plaza, she stopped their forward progress at the first street they came upon. A long look in each direction she gave.

"Are you looking for a cab or something because I can call you an Uber if you want?" Evan asked.

"No, I'm not looking for a ride. I'm just looking. Why? You want to take off?"

"I didn't say that. I just thought maybe you wanted to go home."

"Yeah, that's the last goddamn place I want to be right now. You can go, though. I'll be fine."

"Amanda, come on. I wasn't planning on leaving."

"Okay, great, you're not leaving. Then how far?"

"How far to where? You didn't tell me where we're going."

"How far to wherever you're staying?" she asked as she turned to face him.

Both her words and her eyes weakened him. It was the last thing he expected to hear from her, and it was a look he never expected her to cast upon him. Before he could answer her, a few breaths he had to draw in just to comprehend what had just transpired.

"I'm just a few miles away."

"Good, then lead the way, Evan from Chicago."

* * *

Evan pulled the room key from his pocket. It was noticeably unsteady in his hand. He made a few attempts to get it into the lock. She took the key from him and they entered. He flicked on the light. She looked around.

"I know. Pretty much a dump. It looked a lot better on the Priceline photos."

"This isn't too bad. Trust me. I've been in a lot worse."

Amanda took a seat on the edge of the bed. She leaned back on her hands, crossed her legs, and then reshuffled her hair with a shake of her head. Evan stayed by the door. He was thinking of his own place to sit. He was thinking he really wasn't ready to be with her like this.

"You're looking a little nervous there, Evan from Chicago. Never had a girl in a motel room before?"

Evan shook his head in reply to the question.

"Have you ever even had a girlfriend?"

"I've had a few," Evan replied, taking umbrage at the question.

"University of Chicago girls?"

"No, they were actually from high school."

"That's some drought," Amanda said, and Evan dropped his eyes to the floor. "Okay, I want names."

"Margaret and Janet."

"Damn, those are good girl names. Were they good girls?"

"I guess they were."

"My God, I wish I had your innocence. The world must find you a saint."

"I wish I had your beauty. The world must fall to its knees when you walk out on its stage," Evan retorted, finding a little strength and confidence.

Amanda gave him a small laugh, looked away for a second, and then returned with an answer.

"The world doesn't fall to its knees, Evan. They stare sometimes, yeah. They say things like, 'Hey, we should hook up sometime.' They run their eyes over my tits when I glance away. They call me a slut and a whore behind my back when I don't want to sleep with them. They never ask me what I think about things. They think I'm a goddamn idiot. They never even ask if I'm happy or fucking sad. And that's sad."

"Are you sad a lot?"

"Yeah, I'm sad a lot. But I'm okay with that because for as long as I can remember, I've always felt guilty about being happy. Happiness it comes to my door and I say, 'What the fuck are you doing here? I know you're only going away. So leave and never come back again.' With sadness though, it comes knocking and I give it a big smile and let it right in. I say, 'Welcome, where would you like me to put your bags?' " She glanced away for a second and then added, "Pretty messed up, huh?"

"It can change."

"Yeah, I don't think so. It's all been pre-wired, and I had a pretty shitty electrician."

Her words he found peremptory. And in being so, he didn't

think it would be that much of an abrupt transition if he reached into his pocket for his phone.

"Got a text?" she asked.

"No, not a text. Nobody would be texting me now. I just thought maybe you wanted something to eat. I was going to search for a pizza place. Are you hungry?"

"No, but if you're going to do a search, can you type in 'nearest liquor store' on that phone of yours."

"I have a bottle of Chivas if that's okay."

"You're kidding, right?"

"No."

"Did someone leave it behind?"

"Yeah, how did you know?"

"I think in your world they call it an educated guess. And not that it matters, but is it opened? I like to warn my body first before putting anything inside of it."

"No, the seal is still on it."

"Well, fuck me. Finally, something going my way."

Evan broke from his spot at the door and went over to the bed, where he knelt and flipped up the covers. A moment later he stood back up with the bottle of Chivas in hand.

"I need to get some cups. There's a few in the bathroom. I'll be right back."

"Okay," Amanda answered.

When he returned, Amanda was slipping off the maroon and white hoodie. Underneath, she had on a mauve-colored jersey shirt with white sleeve stripes. In the middle, a large number 4. Above was printed *"ALL of THIS SHIT"* and below that, the lone word

"WHAT?" It was a size smaller than it could have been and accentuated her body gloriously. He read it faster than anyone else would have. She had just finished turning the hoodie back from inside out when he noticed the abscesses on her forearms that always seemed to heal one week later than everyone else. She followed his line of sight and then looked up.

"Something wrong?"

"No, not at all," he said and handed her a cup. He said and then filled it to the top.

"Decide where you're going to sit yet?"

"I was um . . . I was going to just sit over here," Evan said as he turned around and hurried himself to a chair where the dresser and TV were situated.

"Calculated decision I'm assuming. Not too far, not too close."

"I can move somewhere else if you want me to."

"No, you're perfect where you're at."

"Thanks for asking me to come tonight," Evan said as he finally got around to tilting the bottle of Chivas into his own cup.

"It was nice to see a lot of those faces again."

"You don't get to see them a lot?"

"Not since I left The Nucleus. John and heroin have pretty much kept me sequestered from all social activities. Except for work, of course. That they both need for me to keep on the weekly docket."

"Who was that girl blowing out the candles?"

"Tommy's twin sister."

"Does she live here in Buffalo?"

"No, she's in Rochester studying graphic design."

"Jesus, that's got to be devastating for her."

"Yeah, and devastating's probably an understatement. They were really close. Christ, I remember her even sending him a Valentine's Day card. Just goes to show you, Evan from Chicago, never love something too much."

"And why's that?"

"Because while you may think it's perfectly ordered and numbered, it's actually a mean and spiteful universe we live in. As soon as you start loving something more than you should, it gets taken away."

"I can agree with that."

"Okay, enough of all this. My head is starting to hurt again and I need a few things."

"What do you need?"

"First, I need you to pour me another drink. Then after that, I'm thinking I need you to take me to the movies. That way I can live in someone else's sad life for a few hours or so since I'm getting pretty fucking tired of hanging around mine."

"It's already a quarter after two," Evan said after he checked the face of his watch. "They have twenty-four-hour theaters around here?"

"No, they do not. But fortunately, we've all been blessed with the Internet. So, fill up my cup, go get your laptop, and give us a reason to just shut up."

Evan stood and poured her another drink. He then went over to his laptop and began scrolling through a list of movies.

"What would you like to watch?"

"I don't know. Give me something old, maybe something

beautiful, perhaps something blue. Find me uh . . . Find me . . . Let's see. How about Ingmar Bergman's *Wild Strawberries*."

"Okay, that sounds great. One amazing movie coming right up," Evan replied and bought the film for four ninety-nine. The laptop he then hooked to the back of the television screen. After hitting play, he took a seat in the chair by the door. As the movie started, Amanda fixed her eyes on him.

"You're seriously going to sit in the other row?"

"I didn't know where else to—"

"Just come over here. I may scratch and bite, but I don't disfigure."

Evan lifted himself from the chair and walked over to the other side of the bed, where he sat at the edge.

"Uh, Evan from Chicago, I'm sorry, but it's lounge seating in this theater."

At her request, he took off his shoes, lay himself on the bed, and folded his hands in front of him. Amanda gave the movie another few minutes before breaking his interlock and threading her fingers through his. She brought his hand over to her side. She set her head upon his shoulder. She was thinking God just how soft and innocent his touch was and God how this is what it must be like to have a real boyfriend. The movie played on, and she tried hard to get lost in it for fear she would end up loving something again.

Evan was wishing he had a mirror in his other hand. He was wishing he could see how they looked together because he still wasn't sure. Would it look as if they were just two close friends, or would it look like they were simply one and undividable? She squeezed his hand tighter. She brushed her head against him like a cat. And then he thought: *God, it makes no sense for her to be here beside me, and God, she's so beautiful and dangerous.* The movie played on, and he realized that never before had he wanted something more than he wanted her.

BREATHING IS
SUICIDE

I N THE SAME CLOTHES SHE HAD fallen asleep in, Amanda stood in the well of the city bus. The hydraulic brakes made their farewell noise and she hopped off. The methadone clinic had a line out the door, and she placed herself at the end of it. A cigarette lit, her body was twitching for a hit, and her mind was telling her that you know that synthetic shit isn't close to being the fucking same. She was watching her body leaving the line. She was watching her tongue licking her upper lip as the flame from a buck-twenty lighter cooked the score. She had the syringe filling up. She had the needle in a vein, she had a vision of herself floating away. She had peace loaded up. She had heaven in her sight and she had no more pain. But then in the next scene, she had a thought of the night before. She had the credits of the movie rolling by, and she had that boy from Chicago giving her a kiss on the forehead and tucking her in.

"Name?"

"What?"

"Your name? What's your name, sweetie?" the attendant at the clinic asked again.

"Amanda. Amanda Smith."

* * *

Amanda awoke under the covers of her bed. The methadone had delivered her into the arms of Morpheus not long after she had placed her head on the pillow. Not even the fight she had with John after coming home could keep them from closing. Now five hours later, she was awake again. A quick shower and she was back in her room. She dressed and stood in front of the closet mirror. She had on a pink T-shirt with a glittered silver calligraphic font that said: "Breathing is Suicide." She had on stone-washed jeans from the Salvation Army store, and she had on black and white Jada canvas sneakers from eBay. Her head was down, and she was bent at the waist, combing her hair from the back to the front—all the while envisaging she was at the edge of a cliff and staring at all the debris that had already made the trip. And wondering, wondering why she hadn't yet jumped. That question though would have to wait as a text came in.

"What are you doing?" Evan had typed.

"Studying for the MCAT," she texted back.

"Can you meet me at the coffee shop in an hour? There's somewhere I would like to take you."

"Please leave your name and message after the beep."

And that was her final text. She took two steps forward to the mirror to come in for a close-up. Her face had a little color to it, and her lips weren't cracked and dried. There were no red spiderwebs accompanying her emerald-colored eyes. There was no hint that she hadn't slept for days. For once in a long time, she felt like she was that twelve-year-old kid again.

Into the kitchen she went. It didn't startle her at all that John was lying on the floor. She did a wellness check by looking at his chest. It was expanding and collapsing, and so at least she knew he was still alive. On the kitchen table a needle and a spoon, and next to that, a plastic bag with still a few packets of heroin left in it. The plastic bag she picked up and emptied out. The tabs of both packets she undid and tapped the powder out. All that she ever once needed and all that she ever once loved was now in front of her. She leaned over and sucked in a deep breath. She closed her eyes and she made a wish. She exhaled as hard as she could. She exhaled like she had a hundred and one birthday candles to extinguish. The heroin took to the air before going over the edge to settle among the detritus of dust and dirty footprints. *Finally,* she thought, *finally someone who can unfetter these fucking chains.*

* * *

Evan entered the coffee shop and sat at his usual table. This time he was without his laptop. This time he wasn't looking like he needed a friend. Julia grabbed a cup of coffee and brought it over to him. She set it down, stepped back, and folded her arms across her chest.

"Wow, I thought you'd be long gone."

"I decided to stay a little longer."

"Now that's got to be the first time those words have ever been uttered in the city of Buffalo. Mail your letter?"

"Yes, thank you."

"Anything else?"

"No, I'm fine. I'm waiting for someone."

"Well, I'm glad you have a date."

"I didn't say it was a date."

"No, no you didn't. But your cologne did."

"Too much?"

"Not if the two of you are planning on backpacking it for the next few months."

The cook started slamming his hand on the bell. Julia glanced over to the kitchen area.

"Will you stop ringing that goddamn thing before I shove it right up your . . ." Julia began, but stopped short of the last expletive as a few customers had turned their heads. "All right, I gotta go. I'll stop back in a little bit."

"Okay."

Julia hadn't been gone for more than a minute or so when Amanda came into the coffee shop and sat herself across from him.

"Hey," Evan said.

"Hey," Amanda replied with a smile that she hadn't worn in such a long time.

"You doing any better?"

"I don't know. Another piece of me that's been cut out. You

either live with the missing piece, or you just check on out."

"Yeah, I guess that's true."

"So," Amanda said with a slap of her palm on the table, "where are we going?"

"I was thinking the Theodore Roosevelt Inaugural Site."

"Oh, God no. That may have been okay for Madeleine and Janice, but it's definitely not okay with me."

"Margaret and Janet. And it's a National Park Service historic site."

"And being such, it will still be one if you ever return someday."

"Where would you like to go then?"

"Sunday in the Cemetery at Forest Lawn."

"Are you serious?"

"Quite serious. Come on, let's go," Amanda replied and slid her chair out.

Evan was just about to stand up when Julia approached. The waitress took a look at Amanda and widened her eyes.

"Holy shit."

"What?" Amanda questioned.

"Nothing. Nothing at all. You want something?"

"No, I'll call you later. We were just leaving."

"Yeah, about that. Could I have a word with you for a moment?"

"Speak," Amanda replied.

"I kind of wanted to do this without . . ."

"I'll be outside," Evan said. And while Julia was taking a seat next to Amanda, he laid a five-dollar bill down and headed for the door.

"What the fuck are you doing?" Julia started.

"What the hell do you mean?"

"I mean with the kid. What are you two doing?"

"Just hanging out for the afternoon, I guess. Why?"

"He thinks this is a date."

"Yeah, I don't know. Maybe it is."

"That's great. And I'm really happy for the two of you. But if John finds out, he's going to kill him and your death won't be too far behind."

"First, there's nothing to find out. And two, if there ever is, Evan will be back in Chicago before it gets serious."

"That kid is as sweet as pie."

"Fuck you, Julia."

"What the hell did I say?"

"What do you mean what did you say. You're implying that my loser ass is somehow going to corrupt him. You really think that's what I'm like? Maybe I just wanted to know what it's like to spend a few moments with someone who wasn't a junkie or trying to get down my pants. Maybe just someone normal for a goddamn change. But apparently, my best friend doesn't think I'm even worth that."

Amanda arose and shoved her chair back in.

"Come on, Amanda. You know—"

"No, don't worry. My fault. I'll put him back on the shelf after today. Sorry, I forgot. I can only shop in the aisle where they keep the addicts and assholes."

Amanda exited the coffee shop. Evan was on the corner.

"Ready?" he asked.

"Yeah, let's get out of here."

"It was about me, wasn't it?"

"What was about you?"

"What Julia wanted to talk to you about. She doesn't want you to be hanging around with me, right?"

"You got that reversed. She doesn't want you to be hanging around me."

"Why?"

"Because I'm a bad influence, it seems."

"But you make me smile."

"Did you use that line on Madeleine and Janet?"

"No, they weren't bad influences."

* * *

Amanda and Evan were seated on the very last bench of the green and white trolley, staring out at the sun-laden headstones and trees. They had already rolled on by the resting places of Millard Fillmore, Dr. Frederick Cook, Red Jacket, and Shirley Chisholm. Both had barely spoken a word. Both were thinking about their fathers, and both were thinking of each other. The trolley came to another stop on their tour, and the docent spoke into her microphone again.

"To your right, our next famous resident of Forest Lawn is none other than the inimitable funk and soul artist James Ambrose Johnson, Jr. Or, as he is known to the rest of the world, Rick James. Rick James was born to us on February 1st, 1948 in

Buffalo, New York . . ."

"And this is where we get off," Amanda said as she stepped over the legs of Evan and into the aisle.

"I don't think the tour is finished."

"It is for us," she said with a pat of his shoulder.

The docent smiled slightly and turned her body sideways to let Amanda by. From his seat, Evan watched her hop off the trolley. He followed her with his eyes for a moment until realizing she probably wasn't returning. He arose from his seat and gave the docent a chest-high wave. She gave him a wink.

Across the cemetery lawn, he hurried his steps to try and catch up with her. However, she was moving too fast and he had to break into a jog in order to come by her side.

"This isn't the first time you left the tour before it was over, is it?"

"All that education, huh?" she replied.

By the headstone of Rick James they walked by. Amanda brushed her hand over it and continued on. Evan stopped for a moment to read the epitaph: "I'VE HAD IT ALL. I'VE DONE IT ALL. I'VE SEEN IT ALL. IT'S ALL ABOUT LOVE. GOD IS LOVE."

"Do you know who that was?" Evan said as he caught up to her again.

"Yep. Another dead person," she said and then stopped, raising her arm and pointing off in the distance. "That's the Scajaquada Creek. It bisects the park. If we keep following it, it'll let us off on Main Street."

"You come here a lot, don't you?"

"Probably more than any living person should."

"Is your father buried here?" Evan asked.

"Sort of. You know that twelve-year-old girl whom I told you about."

"Yeah."

"Well, she took his ashes and spread them all over this cemetery. Her mom still thinks he's in the urn. Unbeknownst to that woman though, the urn is now a memorial to the Philip Morris company."

"Why did the twelve-year-old girl do that?"

"She didn't want to keep quietly talking to him inside of a fucking living room. She wanted to be able to just walk around and scream to him whenever she wanted to. She was a very cool girl and I miss her a lot. Now stop asking so many goddamn questions and enjoy the dead. They are here for our enjoyment."

For the next two hours, Amanda and Evan spent it like kids at a park. They took photos of each other in various poses at the graves of all of those who had preceded them. They coaxed a couple of cemetery caretakers to dance with them atop the sarcophagus at the George K. Birge memorial as the music from Evan's phone played on. They climbed to the top of the mock aqueduct and tight roped it from one end to the other before jumping off six feet to the ground. They attended a graveside funeral as if they were part of the family. At this city of the dead, they found themselves more alive than they ever remembered having been.

Evan took the lead somewhere in the middle of the race and ended up winning by a good twenty feet. He pulled up in the middle of the bridge and stood between two of the parapets. Hands folded, he was staring down at the pond below. Amanda came walking up. She rested her back against the stone wall of the bridge, and through her blue-tinted aviator sunglasses, looked out in the opposite direction. After finally catching her breath, she spoke.

"I let you win, you know that, right?"

"Yeah, I figured you couldn't be that slow."

To that, Amanda gave him a good crack right in the middle of the back. It turned him around so that they were now looking the same way. He reached out and removed her sunglasses so that he could have a look at her eyes. A step closer she took and opened them wide. They were the most alluring hue of green, and they were so magnetic that he couldn't seem to break free from staring into them. At first, he was just making her uncomfortable, and then it began to really piss her off.

"There. See. I'm not high," she said and relieved the sunglasses from his hand.

"That's not why I wanted to see them."

"Sorry, but that's the only reason anyone has ever wanted to look at them."

"Are you sure? Maybe it's just an excuse they use to see how beautiful they are."

"Yeah, I'm fucking sure," she replied and returned the aviators to her face to hide her eyes once again.

"Where do you get all your shirts?" Evan asked as he moved his eyes to the writing printed across her chest.

"At Positive Approach Press over on Fargo Avenue. I hand

them a slip of paper with the thought of the day, and they hand me back something to wear."

"You really think breathing is suicide?" he questioned.

"Never wear anything you don't have an affiliation with, Evan from Chicago. The first rule of donning printed shirts, whether that be band tees or sayings from inside of your mind."

"You have an affiliation with suicide?"

"You know what they say, don't ya? Fifty percent answer yes, and the other fifty percent are liars. Why? You never think about death?"

"I think about my father's death a lot."

"I mean your own."

"No, I never think about it. Why, do you?"

"Yeah, I think about it all the time," Amanda replied. "I'm alone in a room sitting on the floor. My head is resting on a mattress and my deer eyes are staring up at a filthy ceiling. There's a needle in my arm and a bag of dope right next to me. I believe they call it intrusive thought."

"It doesn't have to end that way."

"No, it doesn't. But it will. It's just not this addiction that haunts me. It's this feeling I've had since I was a little girl. This feeling that I would never grow old."

"You're already a lot older than when you first started feeling that way," Evan answered her.

Amanda slowly churned his reply in her head. She pushed off the wall of the bridge and answered in a distant voice meant more for herself than for him.

"Yeah, I guess I am."

"What?" Evan asked as he left his spot to follow her.

"Nothing. I said let's go. I have a taste for ice cream."

They were walking out of the cemetery when Evan breathed out a laugh, and it made it to her ears.

"What's so funny?"

"I can't believe you put a rose on that guy's coffin."

"Listen, his wife was just standing there with the basket and no one was coming forward. So, I thought I would put an end to the uncomfortable pause that had befallen the graveside party and help everyone out. Why? Did I embarrass you?"

"No, not at all."

"That's good, because I'm not embarrassed to walk around with a guy who gets all of his clothes from the J.C. Penney outlet store."

"I love J.C. Penney."

"Yes, and it shows."

* * *

As they walked in the gloaming, Amanda felt like she was a young girl again and Evan knew that this was the first time he had truly ever fallen in love. She gave him a push into the light rain of a lawn sprinkler. He retaliated by gently tackling her to the parkway grass of an old Victorian house. She sat up and wrapped her arms around her knees. He remained where he fell, pretending to be injured. Looking straight ahead, she saw on the porch an elderly couple sitting so close that a sheet of paper couldn't be fit between. The old man smiled and his wife put her head on his shoulder. It was the first time she ever imagined herself fifty years older, and it was such a long time that she ever believed in a tomorrow. And though she wished it could have been because she had gotten stronger, in all truth she knew it was because of the boy beside her. He alone had injected a new life into her. He was now coursing through her veins, and he was so much easier than heroin.

* * *

The day had left the page and neither had even noticed it. At Parkside Candy, the line was out the door and both took in the scene.

"Have you been here before?" Evan asked.

"Yeah, but it's been a while."

"How long is a while?"

"About ten years."

"God, that is a long time."

"Yeah, I thought I'd never return."

"Why?"

"It's a bit of a story."

"We've got time. The line is moving kind of slow."

"All right. I'll tell it. Fuck, I don't think I've told anyone this. Not even my mother. Anyway, my father and I used to come here religiously every Saturday night. A father and daughter thing, you know. Well, for the last six months of his life he was in a wheelchair. So, every time we came here I had to push him from our house to this place."

"How far was that?"

"A little over three-and-a-half miles."

"That's a long way for a twelve-year-old girl to be pushing someone."

"Yeah, she didn't care, though. She just wanted to be with him."

"So, what happened that you haven't wanted to come back?"

"I didn't say that I didn't want to come back. I just said I thought I would never return. There's a difference," Amanda said, stopping short of letting him know the difference was coming there with someone who gave her the same comfort as her father.

"Okay, sorry. I didn't mean to interrupt."

"It's fine. So anyway, we were in a line as long as this one, and there were some teenage assholes a few people ahead of us. They thought it was fucking funny to see some guy in a wheelchair whose hands are all twisted and whose face is drooped on one side. Every minute or so, they would turn around and contort their hands and faces to imitate him."

"That would have sucked to go through."

"No, it didn't suck for me. I could take it. For my dad, though, yeah. He was a very proud dude whom I knew was more embarrassed for his daughter than he was for himself."

"Did you end up leaving?"

"Fuck no. I walked right up to one of those motherfuckers and asked the tallest one if he had any balls. When he snickered and said, 'Yeah, I have fucking balls,' I kicked him in the crouch as hard as I could. So after he crumpled to the ground, I got down on a knee to bring myself to his level and said, 'You're right. You do have fucking balls.' "

"That's great."

"Yeah, she was great. What I remember most though is walking back and seeing my father laughing. His whole body was shaking, and I had to take out a napkin to wipe his face and chin. But damn, I knew inside he was thinking this girl is going to be okay without me. She is one little tornado who is never going to take shit from anyone."

Amanda closed down hard on her glassy eyes and turned her head to the side. Evan was staring at her while she was counting backward from twenty like she always did to stave off the tears. Just like that day when she was holding her father's hand in the hospital. That day when he finally died. She didn't cry then, and she certainly wasn't going to cry now.

"Hey, we can go if you want."

"No, I'm fine. It was just a story. Everyone's got stories. Nothing fucking special."

"It is—"

"Evan," she said and took hold of his shoulders to turn him so that he faced the counter. "Order. He's waiting for you to give him your order."

"Oh," he said, surprised that they were already at the counter. "I'll have a sundae with fudge topping."

"Peanut butter and chocolate. Two scoops," Amanda added.

"With tax that'll be—" the kid at the counter started to say.

"Twelve forty-seven," Evan said absently as he was reaching in his back pocket for his wallet.

"Yeah, twelve forty-seven," the kid said with a look of bewilderment.

"How in the hell did you know that?" Amanda questioned.

"What?"

"The exact amount."

"Oh, I don't know. It's just multiplication."

"No, Evan, eight times eight is just multiplication. Knowing the total of an order with sales tax is truly disturbing."

"Really?"

"Yes, really. And how do you even know what the Buffalo sales tax rate is? You live in Chicago."

"It's on every bill here."

"Yeah, I guess it is," Amanda replied with a roll of her eyes and then added, "Freak."

"Here's your ice cream," Evan said as he took the two-scoop cone handed to him and gave it to her. "Where do you want to sit?"

Amanda's eyes immediately went to the table where she and her father always sat. When she found it occupied, she began to scan around for another one. The recognition on both ends was immediate, and under her breath, she uttered: "Fuck."

"Did you find a place to sit?"

"You know what. I don't feel like sitting in here. Why don't we just leave and walk with them."

"All right. Whatever you want."

They were a half block down Main Street when past them ran a body who did an exaggerated U-turn, and now stood in front of them. He was scratching at his left arm and he was sweating at the brow and he was all strung out.

"Hey, Amanda. I thought that was you. What's going on?"

"Nothing. Just out for an ice cream cone," she answered.

"You gonna introduce me to your friend?"

"Yeah, sure. Sean, this is Evan. And Evan, Sean, obviously."

"Ellen, cool name, man. Nice to meet you," he said and reached out to shake hands.

Evan gave a glance to Amanda, and she couldn't help but to breathe out a laugh.

"Sean, it's . . . Oh, fucking forget it. Listen, we were just heading home."

"Yeah, I can see that. Could I uh . . . could I have a word with you for a moment?"

"Do you mind? I'll just be a minute." Amanda asked of Evan.

"No, I'm fine. Go ahead."

Amanda handed Evan her ice cream cone and then walked off with Sean. They had gotten no more than ten feet away when he stopped them and popped the question.

"You got any?"

"I'm clean, Sean."

"Yeah, right."

"Believe what the fuck you want to believe."

"Come on, Amanda. I came through for you plenty of times when you needed it. How many times did you and John stop by my place to score and I got you guys what you needed?"

"Sean, if I had any, I would give it to you. Why don't you just go downtown?" Amanda said and then gave a glance to where Evan was standing.

"I'm cashed out."

"Jesus, this shit is like family," Amanda said as she dug a hand into her pocket. "Even when you want nothing to do with it, it still shows up on your doorstep. Here. Twelve bucks. That's all I have."

"Thanks, Amanda. Thanks a lot. You're a lifesaver."

"Can I get back to my ice cream cone now before the whole goddamn thing melts?"

"Sure. Go ahead. It was nice seeing you again."

Amanda returned to Evan. His sundae was still untouched. Her cone had lost its top scoop, and the bottom one was melting down his hand and wrist.

"Sorry, it sort of fell off."

"That's all right," Amanda said as she took her ice cream, which she then brought to a garbage can and tossed in.

"That could have been saved," Evan said after she returned.

"Here's a lesson from the streets for ya. Don't try saving anything that you already know is a mess."

"Can we go back in? I should probably wash this off."

"Yeah, you probably should. Stay here. I'll go get something to clean you up."

Amanda was back in a minute with a handful of napkins and a cup of water. She was wiping the chocolate and peanut butter off of his hands when he brought to her a question.

"How do you know that guy?"

"Do you want the truth, or do you want a good lie?"

"Can I start with the good lie?"

"I used to tutor him in math and he wanted to know if I was still taking students."

"Do you want to leave it at that? I'm okay with it, you know.

Really."

"Fuck, Evan. Can you please just be an asshole for one goddamn moment? It's really quite disconcerting to be with someone so fucking understanding."

"I just didn't want you to think I need to know everything."

"No, you won't get everything. And not because I can't trust you not to judge me, but because it makes me feel ugly. And I'm so tired of feeling ugly. Now, do you mind walking me home? I should probably sleep there since I didn't last night."

"Sure. Of course."

Only a few steps into their walk back to Amanda's apartment, a small smile came to her face, and she shook her head contemplatively.

"You know, of all the drugs they've derived and synthesized, they still haven't come up with the one that they could sell to everybody."

"What would that be?"

"The one that erases your past. Who in the hell wouldn't want to fucking score that."

* * *

On the walk back, there was no room to speak as both were busy replaying vignettes from the last four days. He couldn't remember a better time in his life, and not counting Tommy's memorial, she was thinking the same. He knew he was in love because he couldn't stop smiling every time he pictured her face. He knew he was in love because he now found himself scared that tomorrow would come and she would no longer be there. She was trying to pick out the exact moment when she realized this was the boy whom she would have wanted her father to meet. In all actuality, it probably could have been any one of them. However, she concluded that it was when he called her back and sincerely questioned, "Why does tomorrow always suck?" Except for her dad, anyone else wouldn't have cared enough to ask, and anyone else would have let her keep walking away.

Three blocks left, then two, and finally one. Now both had fifty or so feet for a concluding speech. He was rearranging words and sentences, but nothing seemed to be making sense. She was thinking of bringing perhaps just a simple goodbye with maybe a thank you for the day and ice cream. They arrived at the sidewalk in front of her apartment before either had a chance to figure it all out. At a distance of friends they stood, even after all that had passed between.

"I'd ask you up, but I'm living with someone, a recovering heroin addict as of late, and, according to Julia, no good for you."

"It's okay. I understand. I had a great day."

"Yeah, me too. Fuck, I haven't had one in so long. It felt normal. And that's all I wanted. I deserve that every few years."

"You deserve it more than that. Are we um . . . Are we going to see each other again?" Evan managed to finally get out.

"Evan, you're an extremely smart kid. Think about it. Your date just told you she had a very good day walking around a cemetery with you. You should give her a good hug, kiss her on the cheek, and then run from her as fast as you fucking can."

Prompted, Evan closed the distance between them and put his

arms around her. She felt soft and fragile. She felt like if he held her any tighter she would break. That strawberry scent on her hair he inhaled. It mixed beautifully with the smell of soap and dry grass on her skin. He didn't want to let go but believed that if he didn't, it would scare her to death and she would leave forever. He broke from the embrace, kissed her on the cheek. However, instead of running away as fast as he could, he stayed in place.

Amanda looked at the boy in front of her. Never in her life had she been held so delicately. Julia was right. He was sweet as pie and such a precious thing. The cologne he had put on she would take with her to sleep. That look of innocence in his eyes was terrifying. She knew he wouldn't kiss her. She thought about it for a moment. Never before did she think she had to be brave. She took a step forward, closed her eyes, and hoped he would meet her halfway.

Evan cupped her face with his hands and put his lips to hers. He expected her to press hard, but she had no intention of that. She was gentle with him and she was soft with him and she was the girl she had always wanted to be with someone. Slowly, ever so slowly, she slipped her tongue into his mouth. He reciprocated and followed her step for step. This is what it was like to be with a boy. This she had always dreamed of. But as time moved on she began to hate herself for feeling like this. Life had never been that kind, and certainly, she didn't deserve it. So, instead of ending everything with just one last sweet kiss, she instead bit down hard upon his bottom lip. He pulled back immediately to run a finger over where her teeth had broken skin. At the smear of blood he was staring when she spoke to him.

"Remember this and always this, Evan from Chicago. That first kiss is always the best you'll ever get. Right after that, the two of you will just spend the rest of your lives like vampires, sucking that love from each other until one day there is nothing left."

They were words he didn't want to accept, although the blood she had drawn was irrefutable evidence. He wanted to pull her once again into his arms and tell her that what she had said wasn't always true with everyone she met. It was too late though as she had already started to make her escape. He watched her to the door. He watched her go inside and beyond that. He was thinking she just needed someone to hold her through all of this.

Evan turned around and started to make his way back to the motel. He decided he didn't want to call for a car. He would just walk the three miles and think about that kiss. Upstairs and unbeknownst to both of them, John had been watching their goodbye from the apartment window. His fingers slipped from the curtain, and he took another drink from the bottle of Scotch in his hand.

* * *

Evan was nearing the corner of the block when Emily's father opened the screen door to their house and hurried out. He was walking fast to catch up to the person he had been looking for the last few days. Evan crossed the street and kept heading straight. Not wanting to frighten the kid by coming right up on him, Emily's father closed the distance to within a few houses and then called out.

"Hey, wait up!"

The voice was immediately recognizable, and he thought it best to just ignore the summons and pick up the pace.

"Can you please stop? I'm not going to do anything to you. I just want to talk," he said in a voice just a little louder than before.

Evan gave thought to taking off. The odds though he believed were that he would be caught anyway. So, he put his motion to rest and slowly turned around. Emily's father finished the distance. Evan spoke first.

"I haven't been to the hospital. I haven't seen her."

"I know. I know."

"What do you want then?" Evan asked, his heart beating hard against his chest.

"Emily keeps asking for you. She told me to go out and see if I could find you. She thinks you left to conquer another land."

"How is she doing?"

"She's having surgery the day after tomorrow."

"For what?"

"The tumor in her brain is back. She's had this goddamn disease since she was four. We beat it the first time, but last month her headaches started to return."

"I'm sorry. I don't know what to say."

"Just say you'll stop by before she goes into surgery."

"Yes, of course. I'll be there tomorrow. What are the doctors saying?"

"They're saying this surgery is just to relieve the pressure. They're saying she won't live to see nine. That's pretty fucked up, isn't it? I mean who in the hell doesn't live to see nine years old. Everyone gets to see nine years old, don't they? I mean you, me and even her shithead mother who skipped out on us got to see nine. Her though, the best of the bunch, gets only eight."

"Does Emily know?"

"No, I haven't told her. I mean how in the hell do you tell your daughter she has only a few months to live? Who in the hell has the strength to say those words?" He looked aside for a moment to keep Evan from seeing the tears in his eyes. When he was sure they weren't going to fall, he finished what he had to say. "You know what fucking gets me is to think of all the movies I've watched where some character's been told that he or she has only a few months to live. And not more than five minutes later, that character is dead. I've always thought that was such a big violation of time. But now, I'm starting to believe they got it fucking right because those credits in your life they roll by faster than you ever would think."

All those things Amanda had said about death came rushing into his head. The one though that seemed to be the perfect fit was the one where she had said: "Because it's a mean and spiteful universe we live in. As soon as you start loving something more than you should, it gets taken away." He shook hands with Emily's father. The shake was then a quick embrace. Evan let him leave first, and he had yet to walk a full block when her voice entered into his head again. *Fuck, every time. Every goddamn time I let myself start to enjoy a day, something comes into my life to tap me on the shoulder to say you know better than that.*

L³ = LIVE LOVE AND LEARN

S HE HAD TAKEN THE DECISION to bed with her and in the morning awoke with an immediate resolution. She would leave him today and never look back. That addiction she would break, and with the heroin, she swore to work hard to sever the relationship. From room to room she began her search to see if he was home. With no sign of him anywhere, the anxiety that was making her shake was quickly expelled by a wave of relief that flooded her veins and put her at ease.

From the closet, she pulled out her beige suitcase and set it on the bed. The hard-shell casing was plastered with stickers from concerts she had attended and bands that she still adored. At her dresser, she indiscriminately grabbed handfuls of underwear and handfuls of shirts and tossed them in. Another look in her closet and a few pairs of jeans she added on top of that.

Lastly, she needed a few books, and she needed a few albums to take with. Standing at the five-tiered shelving unit, her fingers tapped over the spines of all her novels like she was playing a piano one-handed. Three books she concluded she would limit herself to. So, in memory of her father, in memory of the one he would always read to her when she was a child, she brought down Antoine de Saint-Exupéry's *The Little Prince*. For the book that still made her feel alive, she picked Anthony Burgess' *A Clockwork Orange*. And then finally, finally for her soul, she grabbed Richard Bach's *Illusions*. The choice of music was not so easy though. The three black plastic crates under her bedroom window were packed tight with all of the vinyl records she had collected. In the end she decided on nothing, and in the end she just took the first two albums from each of the bins.

The suitcase locked, now there were only two items left on her list. The shower she took first as that was the easiest. A dress for the night, that would require a little more thought and that would require a little more time. Standing half-dried with drops of water dripping from her hair, she shuffled through a collection of dated teenage dresses. All were black and all made no sense for a date like this. Ultimately, it was the unpretentious one from prom she finally decided upon. She had just zipped it up in the back when a call came in.

"What time are you coming over?" Julia asked.

"Probably late," she answered. "I'm going out with Evan tonight."

"You're all packed, right?"

"Yep, one suitcase and one smiling face."

"Perfect. That's all you ever fucking need anyway. Did you tell Asshole that you're leaving?"

"No," Amanda replied, pausing afterward to reflect on the finality. "All right, I got to get out of here. Thanks again, Julia."

She tapped the screen to disconnect the call and immediately began to feel a bit of dolefulness. The two years she and John had spent with each other were far from ideal, but they were still two years in the books. The end of anything she understood was never a new beginning until you could forget everything. But unfortunately, right there on the tarmac, she was now remembering. They may have both been jagged puzzle pieces, but for those first six months they were puzzle pieces that perfectly fit together.

She dried her eyes with the towel and then finished drying her hair. The door to the closet she closed and stood there before the full-length mirror. The dress was barely hanging onto her shoulders. Those fifteen pounds she had dropped between then and now left a ton of space between body and cloth. It would have to do. It was all she had to work with. The slam of the front door turned her head and out loud she softly said, "Shit."

In the bedroom doorway, he had one hand high up on the frame, and his body he had listing a bit. He took a glance at the suitcase on the bed and then returned his eyes to hers.

"Taking a little vacation?"

"We need some time apart. I'm going to stay at Julia's for a little while," Amanda said.

"Okay, I'm cool with that. Probably a good idea. Obviously, you're not happy."

"I'm clean, John. I don't need to be around any of that shit right now," she replied.

"Never seen you in a dress, Amanda. Got a date on your first night away?"

"I was just trying it on. Wanted to see if I should even bother taking it with me."

John pushed off the frame and walked over to the bed, where he sat down.

"You're going to stay in touch, right?" he asked.

"Yeah, of course I will."

"You still love me?"

"Don't ask me that now, John. You've had two years to ask and you never did."

"We're from the same cut, Amanda. You know that."

"From the same cut, John? Seriously, that's the best way you can describe our relationship is with a drug metaphor? God, is that so messed up. What the fuck have I done? How could I have invested so much time in you?"

"Come on, Amanda. It wasn't that goddamn bad. We had a lot of good times."

"All of those good times you're referring to came with a needle in our arms. How in the hell is that good?"

"Okay, we sucked then. What the fuck else can I say. Just go."

From his front pocket, John pulled out a plastic baggie and tossed it on the cover of the bed. From his back pocket, he pulled out the paraphernalia. In his head, he still had that picture of Amanda and Evan breaking from a kiss.

"You're really going to be an asshole and shoot that in front of me?"

"Just pretend I'm not here. Seems like you're already halfway there anyway."

He had a packet of heroin in one hand. He had the spoon underneath and ready to receive. Amanda walked a few steps and snatched the packet out of his hand.

"Cut it out. Fuck, why did you have to come home? Five more minutes and I was out of here."

"You really know how to make someone feel completely worthless, Amanda."

"I didn't mean it like that."

"Yeah, you did."

"Christ, John. What do you want from me?"

"Nothing. Nothing at all. Just gimme my shit back and go. I'll wait until you leave."

"No, I don't want you doing it. You need to clean up more than anyone."

"I will. Just once more and that'll be the last."

"Fuck. Here. Take it," she said and threw it at him.

She had the handle of the suitcase in her hand. She had her body two steps from the doorway. She had an image of herself walking out of the apartment and heading toward a new sun.

"I'll always love you, Amanda. You were the best thing for me, and I know I fucked it all up. I'm sorry. Really. Fuck. I'm so sorry."

The suitcase she set down. A sudden change of heart. A sudden change of direction. She walked over to the bed and delivered her body to him. An arm across her knee, she spoke with eyes lowered and the realization of defeat.

"Can I go first?"

"Yeah," he said, and the grains they fell from heaven to quickly pile up on the spoon.

* * *

Evan entered the hospital room with the best smile he could put on. Upon seeing his face, Emily quickly rolled to the other side and pulled the bedsheet over her head. Evan immediately shifted a look to her father. He was sitting on a chair by the window. He had it turned so he had both Emily and her scary machines in the same frame. After removing from his mouth the fingernail he was biting on, he lifted a few strands of his hair. Evan understood and continued on to her bed, but not before having to make one stop. And that one stop was to pick up the tiara that had been tossed to the floor. He stooped down, took it into his hands, and now stood at her edge.

"Princess Emily."

"Go away," she answered in a voice muffled by the sheet.

"Wherefore, princess?" he replied, although the phrasing sounded so inane to him considering what she was going through.

"Please just go away. I don't want to see you."

Evan placed his eyes back on her father, and he nodded for him to continue on.

"I brought you something," Evan said and held out the small gift-wrapped box he had brought.

"I don't want it. I don't want it at all," she answered in a teary voice.

Evan set the present on the table beside Emily. He then lowered the bedrail and sat down. A gentle hand he placed on her shoulder and she edged closer to the other side.

"Evan, please just leave. I don't want you to see me like this."

"Although the order given, I cannot abandon the princess."

"How can I be a princess anymore? They have taken all of my hair away."

Her reply was a poisoned arrowhead that found the weakest part of him, and for a moment, he found himself paralyzed and without anything in return to say. Finally, after a long pause, he became strong again and answered her.

"Have they taken thy heart?"

"No, of course not," she said.

"Then a princess you still are. For it's what is in your heart that makes you one."

"Are you sure?" she asked.

"By my sword."

That troth seemed enough for her. Slowly she rolled over and slowly she sat herself up. Over her hospital gown, she was wearing a knee-length cotton shirt with a bunny on the tips of its toes reaching up to a chalkboard. All around were blurry-eyed math equations. The only one clear and discernible was the one that read: "L^3 = Live Love and Learn."

"I am sorry, Lord Evan. I am ugly," she said in the most humble of apologies.

"By all the stars above I swear you are still the most beautiful girl in the world."

With that, he picked up the tiara that he had set on the bed. She tilted her head toward him, and he set the diadem upon it. The coronation he followed with a kiss to the back of her hand. Her face reddened a bit, and her lips curved up into a smile that made both him and her father feel the pain of life.

"I am so afraid, Evan."

"I know," he answered with a nod. "That is why I have brought the knights with me."

"I don't see them."

"Outside they are gathered," he replied and held out his hand for her to take. "Come with me and I'll show them to you."

Her little hand she sheltered inside of his, and he eased her to the floor. The IV stand he took hold of and led the way to the window. Her father slid his chair off to the side to clear a path, and her father closed his eyes tight for a moment to hold back all of those tears that were rushing forth. Evan parted the curtains, went to a knee, and then ushered her forward. An arm he wrapped around her tiny waist as she was scanning the parking area.

"I only see cars."

"Close your eyes." So tight she shuttered them that to her, it seemed as if she had floated up to the heavens and was staring down at the starry universe. "Now open them and look outside, Princess."

Emily slowly lifted her lids and returned back to earth. Outside now, instead of a parking area, she saw a verdant countryside spotted with hillocks. And on the land were gathered small groupings of her knights. Some were on white horses, and some were in formation. All were wearing chainmail armor, and all had on white tunics with a red cross. They had on grieves to cover their legs and they had on iron helmets to protect their faces. Swords drawn, but at their sides, they seemed to be waiting for others to arrive.

"What do you see?" Evan asked of her.

"Hundreds. I see hundreds of them."

"Is that it? Only hundreds?"

"Yes," Emily nodded.

"Close your eyes again and squeeze my hand as tight as you can."

She did as requested, and this time when Evan told her to open her eyes once more, the countryside was filled with an entire cavalry. Not a speck of grass could she see, nor could she tell where the land began or where it ceased.

"And now?"

"Thousands and thousands, Lord Evan. Are they all for me?"

"Yes, my dear Princess. All have come just to be by your side."

"How did they know?" Emily asked as she took her eyes away from the window and looked at him.

"I sent a letter out yesterday, and in it I told them that the princess was in need of their assistance."

"I love you, Lord Evan," she said and threw her arms around him.

"I love you, too," Evan said softly into her ear.

A kiss on the cheek she then gave him and withdrew from the embrace. Into his eyes she looked and asked, "Will you be here tomorrow?"

"Oh, my dearest princess, all the gold in the world could not buy my absence."

Evan came to his feet and was just about to walk her back to the bed when he realized now was the time to write himself out of the script. After all, both father and daughter had come so far, and really he was just a houseguest. Her little hand he took and fit it into her dad's. And as they folded over each other, to him, it seemed like two perfectly matched puzzle pieces.

Emily's father rose from the chair and Evan stepped aside. The king led the princess back to where she lay, and Evan turned to the window. The parking area may have been full of cars and beyond that a church and apartment rentals, but there was no reason not to believe for just those few seconds while she was looking out, that it wasn't full of armored knights and white steeds.

In silence, they both sat while the princess began her journey to the land of nod. Sam was tucked tight in her arms, and her jeweled tiara was still fit to her head. Evan was thinking that perhaps, okay just maybe, if there is a heaven then his father is probably smiling down upon him. He was thinking that of all the accomplishments he had achieved in this life, this would have made his father the proudest. Sitting there, he had come to finally realize why his father had become a high school teacher instead of setting out to rule the world. After all, you can add up all of your achievements, and in the end, isn't it just the smallest of kind gestures that truly make you a king.

Emily's father had her life streaming through his head. It wasn't continuous and it wasn't at all chronological. It wasn't of all the trips to the doctors they had taken and it wasn't of all the times he had to hold her through the chemotherapy. There were vignettes of Christmas mornings and there were vignettes of him reading to her in bed. There were the recollections of all the cute things she had said, and there were the memories of her bringing frozen waffles to his morning bed. And of course, there were all the times that they had spent at the park. Never once did she forget to tell him that she loved him when he dropped her off at the daycare center, and never once did she forget to jump into his arms when he picked her up. They were three. Him, her, and Sam. And three was always just a perfect prime number. *Go back in time. Pick any hamlet, pick any town. God, I swear, no one ever, has ever loved anyone more than I love you, my dear Emily.*

* * *

Emily's father was the first to rise. He was the first to go over to her bed. A kiss on her cheek and a pat of Sam's head. The bedsheet he pulled up to her neck and then he checked the IV line in her wrist.

"She's asleep. Come on. I'll walk you out," he said to Evan in a whispered voice.

Evan stood and followed him into the hallway. The path was busy with nurses, doctors, and residents. They barely noticed these two that had come off the battlefield. They of course had their own campaigns to contend with. At the elevator, Evan turned around and Emily's father immediately spoke.

"That was an amazing thing you did back there."

"If it's okay with you, I would like to be here tomorrow."

"They start prepping her at nine-thirty," he said and then reached around Evan to press the button to the elevator.

"How do you even do it? How do you even take one minute of this?"

"Because that minute may just be all I have left," he said.

Evan nodded and watched him leave. One of the girls he had seen a few days before shot past and kept on running. Room 413, it was easy to remember. The chime of the elevator rang, and the door spread its silver metal wings. He would forgo his departure and take a walk over to surprise her. The bed was made when he stepped in. The curtain was parted wide, and the sun was laying down a golden ribbon across the floor. There were no machines standing guard, and there were no balloons or get-well cards. Maybe she was moved, perhaps she had already been discharged. He took a few steps farther in. A rake of his hand through his hair and then under the bed he noticed it.

"Can I help you?" a nurse said as she stood in the frame of the doorway. She said as Evan was getting up from his knees.

"I was just . . . I was just looking for the girl who was in this room," Evan answered as he now held the magenta wig in both of his hands.

"Are you related to her?"

"A friend, I guess."

"You'll need to talk to her family," she said peremptorily and then left.

Evan hurried his steps and caught up with her down the hall. He then walked ahead and stopped in her path to block any further advance.

"Why do I need to talk to her family?" Evan asked.

"What did you mean by 'A friend, I guess.'?"

"I've been here a few times visiting Emily Jones and I've seen her around. She gave me her room number I guess as some sort of joke, but I wanted to stop by to say hello. This wig, it was hers."

"Okay," the nurse said, looking off to the left for a moment and then sucking in a deep breath. "Marissa died last night."

"No, we're talking about a different girl then. You must know who she is. She's about five-four, maybe fourteen years old. Last time I saw her, she was—"

"Please, don't make this any harder for either of us. Everyone in this hospital knows that wig."

* * *

Amanda came into Buffalo Central Terminal walking erratically and dragging a suitcase behind her. It didn't even strike her as odd that she was moving against the tide as throngs of people kept filing past her. Evan was sitting down on a bench just in front of the old station clock. His legs were crossed, the top button from his white dress shirt undone, and a bow tie clipped to his left lapel. It was difficult to watch her as she neared and so he bowed his head to have a look at the marble floor.

"Whew, that's a long goddamn walk. They need to move this place closer to the road."

"Looks like you're going somewhere," Evan replied as he looked up.

"Yes, I am, sir. To a party. And I've brought a change of clothes in case it goes a little long."

"The party was three hours ago. You're a little late."

"Well, that sucks," she said, standing her suitcase up on its wheels and letting go of the handle.

"Yeah, it does suck."

Amanda stepped between his legs. She put her fingers up to his neck and straightened out his collar.

"Did anyone ever tell you that you look so handsome in a tux?"

"No."

"Well, they should have."

She then leaned in to kiss him. He turned his head and her lips landed on his cheek.

"Well, fuck, I didn't want to kiss you either."

"Do you want to tell me where you've been?"

"Packing. And packing takes a long time."

"It looks like you've been doing more than packing."

"Well, Mr. Fucking Inquisitive, for your information, I was also in the process of dissolving a relationship, which may have contributed a little to my tardiness."

"Did you shoot up with him?"

"Hmm. Let me see. Yes. Yes, I did. But there is good news."

"And what's that?"

"I didn't sleep with him."

"I wish you would have instead of shooting up with him. That I could have understood. That I could have forgiven you for."

"Forgive me? For fucking what? I'm a junkie, Evan from Chicago. You are well aware of that. We have our good days, and we have our bad days. And today was a bad day, and I was not good."

"Why? I thought you had quit."

"Because I felt fucking sad and that shit is the only thing that makes me happy. That's why."

"I don't make you happy?"

"Truth?"

"Yeah, truth."

"You do make me happy. But heroin takes me to heaven. And do you know what that means?"

"No, what does it mean?"

"It means that in a contest to see who makes Amanda the happiest, you are going up against God. And you don't stand a fucking chance. No one stands a fucking chance."

An intermission was granted to both of them as a security guard walked up. Evan nodded his head to acknowledge his arrival. Amanda gave him a big semicircle wave of her hand along with a puckish smile.

"Hey there, Mr. Policeman," she said.

"Hi there, Miss," he answered her and then turned to the more sober of the two. "You have ten minutes. We're closing soon."

"Okay," Evan replied.

"Is she gonna be all right?" he asked of Evan.

"She can hear you, and yes, she is gonna be just fine."

Evan gave the security guard a nod of assurance, and the security guard took leave of the two kids.

"We should go."

"I'm not going anywhere. I'm taking the next train right on out of this goddamn place."

"It's not a real train station, Amanda," Evan answered somewhat angrily. "It's been abandoned for a while now."

"Well, who the fuck does that? Who keeps something around that's completely goddamn useless?"

"People who loved things they once saw as beautiful. Come on, they're closing. We really have to go."

* * *

Amanda and Evan were standing on a street just outside the train station. He had his hands in his pocket. He was looking around, looking at anything but her. She had her suitcase in front of her. She had a cigarette between her lips. She was trying to hold steady in the warm breeze of the night.

"I'm going to call you a car."

"The fuck you are."

"Come on, Amanda. Just go to Julia's, and we'll talk about this tomorrow. Okay?"

She took her last drag of the Marlboro Red. She gave him her middle finger. She started to walk off. He caught up and began walking beside her.

"Where are you going to go? There's nowhere to go."

"Now that's the smartest thing I've heard come from your mouth, mathematician boy."

"Please, just stop all of this. I'm in love with you, okay."

Those words stopped her immediately. Those words had her giving him a good slap across the face.

"Don't ever fucking say that to me again. Ever. Do you hear me?"

"Yeah, I hear you."

"Good, because anyone who has ever said that to me has either died on me, abandoned me, or fucked me over."

"I don't know what you want from me."

"Take me home with you."

"No, not like this. I can't. You'll never get better with someone always giving in to what you want."

"201 Parkdale."

"What is that?"

"Julia's goddamn address. That's what it is. Call a fucking Uber."

* * *

The faint lights that loitered on after the park had closed always cast a ghostly white all about the place that made it more reminiscent of a late-night horror film than a recreational area. That alone would have brought a chill to the skin of anyone else. But tonight, as she dragged her suitcase behind on the winding asphalt path, she wasn't the least bit afraid. Her demons, they weren't in movie scenes and they weren't in newspaper clippings. They were in her head and they were in her veins, and those were the types that were next to impossible to escape.

Destination finally reached, she fit her body between the chains of a swing and sat down on the worn black leather seat. The ankle strap ballerina flats she felt ridiculous in she undid and plowed her toes into the sand. She then wrapped her arms around herself to ease the cramps and make herself warm, even though the night air was hanging around seventy-eight. She was never a cutter, but oh boy, how wondrous she determined would it be to just shred her wrists and bleed out all of this fucking pain. Lids shuttered tight and body slowly rocking, she began to softly chant: "You can leave, you can leave, you can leave. I know you can fucking leave." After a few minutes though, she realized she wasn't strong enough and probably would never be.

To the children's area she cast a look. It reminded her of all the times her father had taken her there to play. It was a trip back to when life was pure and innocent. It was a trip back to when she had nothing at all on her mind but the moment she was living in. A short slide down into the waiting arms of her father. A day of water balloon fights and a day of building snowmen. But she wasn't more than a moment into the reverie when the thought struck her that innocence and the knowledge of it cannot coexist, for they are incapable of occupying the same fucking space in time. For once you become cognizant of its existence, you are no longer capable of possessing it.

She lifted the hem of her dress to wipe the sweat off of her forehead. She was cold and at the same time burning up inside. That didn't bother her, though. That was okay. All those things that used to make her sick and tremble now she welcomed without regret.

The sound of water turned her head, and at the fountain, she saw him take a drink and then spray it to the ground. The sight of him always knotted her stomach and made her want to wretch. She hated his voice, she hated his smell, she hated his face. He made her feel little, he made her feel dirty, and he made her feel like anything but a human being. His gym shoes were untied, his khaki shorts were wrinkled, and though he was thin, his printed shirt of palm trees bulged out from his distended belly. She always wondered about his age. He could have crossed over fifty a few years ago, but he also could have been just an elderly thirty-five. And it always sickened her to think that of all the beautiful things in the world she could have subjugated herself to, it was this ugly man to whom she had become enslaved.

"Still pissed at me?" he said as he took the swing beside her.

"Of course I'm still fucking pissed."

"Understandable, but I still wasn't the one who sold it to Tommy." She said nothing. He glanced at her suitcase. "You get kicked out?"

"Relocating."

"That's good. I always thought you were better off without John. He just uses people."

"Yeah, well, you're two years too fucking late with that advice."

"I don't think I've ever seen you in a dress," he commented as his eyes walked from her legs to her chest and then finally to her face. "You look really nice in one, you know that?"

"Everything else was at the cleaners. Did you bring it?"

"Yeah, I got it."

Amanda reached over to her suitcase, and from inside the travel tag took out the twenty-dollar bill she had hidden there. The dealer gave a quick scan of the area before reaching in his front pocket and bringing out a zip lock bag of heroin packets. Amanda checked the contents and realized there was more in there than her money could buy.

"I only have twenty. I told you that when I called."

"The bag is a hundred, Amanda. You didn't think I'd do a delivery in the middle of the night for twenty bucks, did you?"

"And you didn't think I would fuck you for the remaining eighty, did ya?"

"We can always negotiate for the rest of it," he said as he placed a hand upon her knee.

"You really thought I would fuck you for it, didn't you? That's why you said you'd meet me out here, right?"

"I thought there was a good possibility," he replied and slid his hand a little higher until it disappeared under her dress and stopped on her upper thigh.

"You go a millimeter higher and I'll scream rape."

He withdrew his hand, and just as she thought he would back off, he grabbed her cheeks and squeezed so hard that it felt like her teeth were cutting flesh.

"Listen, little girl, I could do whatever the hell I wanted with you right now. And even if someone came, what story do you think they would believe? The one where I was forcing myself upon a young, innocent girl, or the one where it was just another junkie giving up her goodie bag for a score."

In that, he let go of her cheeks, and she drew in a deep breath while pushing her palms against the sides of her head.

"Fucking pathetic. Oh my God, how fucking pathetic."

"I'm fucking pathetic?"

"No, you're not the one who's fucking pathetic. It's me. I'm the one. Jesus Christ, I'm the one. I'm the one. I'm the one."

"Fuck, you really are messed up, aren't you? And I just don't mean from the heroin."

"Yeah," she said, barely managing to even utter that one lone word.

She was staring vacantly down at the sand when she felt the twenty being relieved from her hand. She was wishing she was dead when he was standing up. She was wishing she was dead when he was throwing the two packets of heroin at her feet.

"Oh, and Amanda, don't do all of it. It's wicked shit."

He was gone, and she was alone again. She was thinking of just snorting it all. She was thinking that maybe the overdose would take up a line or two on page twenty-three in *The Buffalo News*. On second thought, she decided it couldn't be here. It couldn't be where the ghosts of her and her father still roamed. She got off the swing and grabbed her suitcase. No, it had to be where it was destined to be.

PLAIN BLUE FEATHER HOSPITAL GOWN

EVAN GRABBED THE HANDLE to the door of the coffee shop. The deadbolt rattled against the strike jamb. On the side glass, the sign said it wouldn't open until eight, and by his watch, it was 7:41 a.m. Stepping closer, he pressed his face to the window and tried to espy a look in. For a moment, it looked like no one had yet arrived until he met Julia's eyes around the area of the coffee bar. She held up an index finger, and within a minute, unlocked the door and moved her body between it and the frame.

"Hey, what's going on? We don't open for another fifteen minutes, but you can come in if you want," she said, stepping aside to allow him room to enter.

"No, that's okay. I have to be somewhere. I just wanted to see how Amanda is doing."

"I wouldn't know how she's doing."

"She didn't go to your place last night?"

"No, she told me she was going out with you and would come over after that. I just figured she probably ended up spending the night by you."

"We got into a fight. I called her a car and gave the driver your address."

"How the fuck are you two fighting? You guys just met."

"She shot up with John yesterday afternoon and I was a little upset about it."

"Oh, fuck. I'm gonna call her." Julia took a phone out of her pocket. She dialed Amanda's number a few times but only got her voicemail. "Shit, we got to find her."

"I can't. I have to be at the hospital."

"For what?"

"It's a long story. I just have to be there."

"What time?"

"I have to be there by nine-thirty."

"It's not even eight. Just go to her apartment with me. I hate that prick, and who knows what's gonna happen if I go there alone."

Evan inhaled a deep breath and looked down both directions of the sidewalk while he contemplated the change in plans.

"Just her apartment. That's the only stop you have to make."

"Okay," he replied after giving it one more thought and then not another.

Virginia Austin

* * *

Julia was out the door of the car just as it came to a stop. She was halfway up the entranceway before Evan had even set a foot onto the street. In vain, she twisted the knob a few times before pressing in the buzzer and holding it there. When a reply didn't come, she started pressing the other buzzers there.

"Call her," Julia said with urgency as Evan stepped up behind her.

"Voicemail," Evan replied before he had even pressed the screen to end the call.

"Goddammit," she said with a long exhale. "All right, you stay here. I'm going to run around to the back. Maybe they left the door on the back porch open. If you get in, just call me."

"I don't have your number."

"Shit, that's right. Give me yours and I'll call it right now."

Julia called and was already around the corner of the apartment building when the front door opened. Standing there was the old woman in her morning robe, her rabbit tucked under one arm.

"We're here to see Amanda. She wouldn't answer." The old woman said nothing. "We just want to see if she's okay."

She let Evan in. He watched her climb the stairs to the second floor. He heard a door to an apartment open and close. A call to Julia he gave and remained where he was.

"How the hell did you get in?" she asked after arriving back.

"Some old lady who lives here."

"Okay, let's go."

They ran the stairs up. Julia tried the doorknob and then began

216

to knock.

"Amanda. It's Julia. Come on, open the door. I just want to see if you're all right." Her hand she turned into a fist and now began pounding. "Goddammit, Amanda. Why do people always have to go through this shit for you?"

She finally stopped. She turned around and put her back against the door.

"Fuck."

"What do you want to do?" Evan asked.

"Break it fucking down. That's what I want to do."

"I can give it a try."

"No, I'll do it. I'm getting good at this. Hell, if this isn't reminiscent of the shit I just went through a week and a half ago."

Julia had just pushed off the door with her foot when the apartment door down the hall opened. The old lady stepped out. She had the rabbit still in an arm, but this time she had a key in her unencumbered hand.

"Thank you," Evan said after he walked over.

* * *

There was nothing too unusual about the living room as Julia and Evan entered. The television was on. The June Christmas tree was lit. There was a scattering of beer cans on the coffee table. There was an empty bottle of vodka on the floor. All were as Julia had remembered it before she and John had become estranged.

Julia and Evan started walking toward the back of the apartment. They stopped near the bedroom door. Julia looked into the kitchen. Evan checked the bathroom and shook his head.

"Well, that leaves the bedroom. Ready?"

Evan nodded and Julia put a hand on the knob. Both expected it to be locked, but it opened with no resistance. The light from the hallway followed Julia in as she opened the door to the darkened twelve-by-ten bedroom. It immediately gave her a view of John. He was sitting on the floor with his head thrown back on the mattress cover. His eyes were open wide, staring at the nicotine-stained ceiling. He had both arms unfurled at his side, one with a needle still jabbed into his forearm like a dart with no wing flights. Just above that, he had an armband of black around his bicep from the belt that was used to tie him off. There was no need to come to his side to find a pulse or place a wet finger to his lips. Even from where she stood, it was obvious he had left hours ago, hitchhiking now on an unmarked road with the rest of the newly deceased.

"He's fucking dead," she said and then stepped aside so Evan could enter and have a look at death for himself.

"Christ," Evan commented, the only word he could manage in his next breath.

"I'm going to go to the park. You stay here in case she comes back."

"Okay," Evan said.

"And if she does, don't let her see him. That's all she fucking needs."

"No, I'll keep her in the living room or something."

"Good. That's good. All right. Call me if she returns."

Julia left for the front door, and Evan locked his hands over his head. He was now alone with John, and while he didn't want another look, he couldn't keep his eyes from wandering on over. And there, as he saw death once again, Amanda's description of her own seemed to ironically fit for the one she had lived with. He finally turned away and walked over to the window to part the curtains and let the sun have a look of its own. It was then that he saw her. It was there between the wall and the bed that he found her wedged, looking like a rag doll someone had tossed off the bed.

* * *

The EMTs lifted the body with no particular reverence and placed it on the stretcher. Evan combed a hand through his hair and turned aside. That was as far as he could follow the dead. He took one last deep breath and then tried to exhale out all the thoughts he had inside of his head. Julia was still at the bedroom window. Across the street, she was watching two girls and a little boy. The girls they couldn't have been any older than twelve. The girls they were sitting behind a lemonade stand. The little boy he was running around a lawn trying to give his puppy dog a kiss and a hug. Everything seemed in slow motion from where she stood, but she understood those moments they drive away faster than you think. Those moments she knew they leave with nothing except a look back in a rearview mirror. In her mind, she kept repeating: *Don't grow older, don't grow older, don't grow older. All that comes after will only disappoint. All those dreams you believe in now; well, they're nothing but a sad fucking mirage.*

"Nothing. The place is clean," one of the policemen said as he entered back into the bedroom. "They must have used all they had."

"So," the second of the officers began, "to get this straight again, both of you just showed up here. Neither of you was looking to score, huh? Just two superheroes who happened to be in the neighborhood."

"Yeah, that's right. Two shitty superheroes if you really think about it," Julia said as she let the curtain slip from her fingers and then turned around. "Can I go now? You should have let me ride in the ambulance."

"I told you already. Narcotics is gonna want to talk to you. Now just hang out here until they arrive."

"That's just bullshit," Julia replied. "I want to go to the hospital. You can't keep me from seeing her."

"Uh yeah, under these circumstances, we actually can. It's either that or the two of you can join us on a trip back to the station."

"Neither of you cares, do you? I didn't even like the guy and I'm fucking sad."

"We see this almost every day now."

"Yeah, I don't doubt that. But did it ever cross your minds that those who are left behind only see it once? And after that, they don't see anything ever again."

"We're going to be in the squad filling out some paperwork. Don't get any ideas about leaving through the back."

* * *

The number in pre-op came to five. In the room: a nurse, an anesthesiologist, a father, a little girl, and a stuffed bunny who was being squeezed for dear life. A reprieve of another fifteen minutes had been granted to allow for the arrival of the last passenger on this ride. Two were checking their devices of time. The other three had their eyes fixed on the door, praying that it would open.

"We're going to begin sedation," the nurse said as her watch crossed beyond nine forty-five.

"No, please don't. He's coming. I know he is," Emily entreated. She then raised her little hand and spread all of her fingers apart for perhaps a reprieve of five minutes more. This time though, the nurse ignored the request and looked over to her father.

"Sir, we really have to begin. The doctors are already prepped. We have to get her into the OR."

"Daddy, don't let them put me to sleep. I just want to see Evan."

He went straight to his daughter's eyes, and the tears in them felt like a hand had taken hold of his heart and was squeezing it tight.

"What are a few more minutes going to matter? Look at her. She can't go in like this."

"It's nearing ten. We really have to start," the nurse replied and then nodded to the anesthesiologist.

The IV line from the port in Emily's wrist was disconnected. A small stream squirted out of the syringe. The needle pushed into the tube, and as a thumb touched the plunger, the announcement was made.

"Starting the Versed."

"No, no," Emily said as she wrested her wrist from the grip of the anesthesiologist and hid it underneath her body. "Sam, tell them. Tell them Evan's coming."

The nurse came in to assist. She took hold of Emily's forearm. She lightly pulled the first few times, and then yanked hard on the third to bring it back out from underneath the little girl's body. That last tug was enough for Emily's father. The nurse's wrist he cuffed until her fingers separated.

"Do I need to call someone?" the nurse said.

"No, you don't need to call anyone. What you need to do is give me and my daughter a minute or two before I take that needle out of her hand and jab into your own goddamn arm. You got that?"

Both the nurse and the anesthesiologist backed away.

"Emily, please just calm down, okay. Evan will be here when you come out of surgery."

"I don't think I'm coming back, Daddy."

"Oh, God, sweetheart, don't say that. Of course you are coming back."

"Are you sure?"

"Yes, I'm sure. I'm one hundred percent sure."

"Can I talk to Sam for a second, Daddy?"

"Absolutely."

"Sam, I love you so much. You've been my best friend for so long. I'm so sorry I was so sick sometimes that I couldn't play with you. If I don't see you again, I'll meet you in heaven. Right by the willow tree we talked about, okay?"

With the help of Emily's hand, the bunny nodded his head. Her father leaned over and hugged the two of them tight. He was trying so hard not to tremble and cry. He was trying so hard not to shatter and break. He kissed her on the forehead. He kissed her on the cheek. She handed over the stuffed animal to him, and then she held out her wrist for the anesthesiologist to take. The Versed was started. A moment later she was no longer with them. The doors to the OR swung open, and under heaven's spotlights, they wheeled in the little girl wearing only a plain blue feather hospital gown. The number in pre-op was now one. In the room sat only Sam.

* * *

Evan was situated in the middle of the backseat. He was sitting forward, drained and disquieted. The first ten minutes had them speeding down the highway with open pockets of asphalt ahead. Now they were at a standstill with nothing but cars on all sides. He took another look at his watch. It told him he was now a little more than five hours from when he should have been there.

"What's going on?" he asked.

The driver tapped the screen of the phone on a dashboard mount. It displayed an icon of two vehicles meeting head-on, and he relayed this to his passenger.

"There's an accident up ahead."

Evan fell back, and soon afterward, an ambulance came

screaming down the shoulder and passed them by. That was followed by two state cop cars, another ambulance, and then overhead an Air Evac helicopter. The driver put on his headphones, and Evan kept checking his watch.

"How far are we from Chisholm?" Evan said and then had to repeat himself two more times before having to shake the shoulder of the driver.

"What?" the driver asked after removing one of his earbuds.

"How far are we from Chisholm?"

"One point three miles," the driver replied after tapping his phone a few times.

"I'm getting out," Evan said as he took hold of the door handle.

"I wouldn't recommend that. We're in the middle of a highway."

"No one's moving. What could possibly happen?"

Evan never waited for an answer. He had the door opened and slammed shut before he could hear: "Hey, kid, get the hell back in the car!" He was across one lane and then another. He was over the concrete barrier and he was sidestepping the embankment down to a city street. Into his phone, he tapped the hospital's address to find the shortest path.

* * *

Evan was still in a trot when he hit the hospital parking lot. That trot became a fast walk as he closed in on the entrance. Finally, he stopped to catch his breath and reassemble. His shirt he lifted up and put his face into it. A hand he combed through his hair to get the sodden strands out of his eyes. He moved forward again and was at the front doors of the hospital. They opened and invited him in as if they had been expecting his arrival. He was just about to step through when out the corner of an eye he spotted Emily's father sitting on a bench. He was leaned over. He was staring at the ground. He had the stuffed bunny in his hands, and he was slowly rotating it around.

"Sorry I'm late," Evan said after walking over. "Something came up this morning and I couldn't leave."

"That's okay," Emily's father said without looking up. And after patting a hand on the bench, he added, "I'm just glad you came."

Evan took a seat beside the man. There he decided it best to just wait for Emily's father to speak again. However, when enough time had passed, and the silence was becoming uncomfortable, he figured that perhaps he was the one who should say something.

"Have you had any updates?"

"Nah, no updates."

"Do you want me to go in and check how everything is going?" Evan said as he leaned forward, placed his elbows on his knees, and folded his hands together.

"That won't be necessary."

"They're done already?"

"Yeah, they're done," Emily's father replied and then twirled the bunny one last time so that its eyes were now looking at him.

"Can I go see her?"

"I'm not sure where she's at right now."

"I would think ICU probably, right?"

"No, she's not in ICU," he answered with a shake of his head.

"Where else would they bring her? I don't think they would take her back to her room."

"Probably not."

"I don't understand. If she's not in the ICU, and not in her room, where would she be?"

For the first time in the conversation, Emily's father lifted his head and looked over to Evan. His eyes were bloodshot. They were piercing and they were enraged.

"I don't know. You tell me. Just where in the hell do they take children after they've let the father have one last look?"

A chill shot through Evan as if summer had become winter. He visibly shook and now he was finding it hard to breathe.

"No. God, no."

"I swear, I just pray you live a long fucking life so that this day can keep repeating itself over and over inside of your head. I want this pain to follow you till your dying breath. All you had to do was show up and see her. What possibly could have been so goddamn important that you couldn't make it here before she went in for surgery? She did everything she could to keep them from putting her under because she was so sure you would come."

Evan put his hands to his temples and pushed in like he was squeezing it with a vise. He was crying audibly. He was working hard to get his next words out through the maelstrom.

"I couldn't . . . I couldn't come. You don't understand . . . I was—"

"There's nothing to fucking understand. She's dead, and the

last thing she had on her mind while she was alive was utter disappointment. Life let her down and then so did you. No wonder why she had no will to hang on."

"Don't say that."

"Fuck, does it sicken me to be near you."

Emily's father stood up. He set down the bunny where he had been sitting and started to walk away.

"Please don't leave Sam here. Please."

"He's yours now," Emily's father said after coming to a stop and turning back. "Oh, and don't even fucking think of coming to the wake or funeral. Because if you do, you won't even be recognizable after I finish with you."

Those last words they were like a cannonball shot to the gut. They emptied all the air out of his lungs, and now he was finding it hard to draw in another breath to replace what had been lost. He began to feel heavy. He began to feel the density of it all. A complete gravitational collapse from which there was no escape. And then all of a sudden everything went black, and suddenly he felt like there was nothing there at all except for him. There he could see himself sitting on that bench forever. A single reason he couldn't come up with for wanting to move on. The bunny he took into his hands and rotated it so he could see the face. A twist of the hospital admittance band on its wrist and now the words "CHISHOLM PARK - PATIENT - EMILY JONES" read back like an epitaph.

* * *

With Sam in his hands, Evan was standing on the other side of the security rail looking far off in the distance. He couldn't have been more than a few feet from the escarpment. White mist like white smoke was rising up as if the water was burning. The sun was still a foot from the horizon. It wasn't round but more like an explosion in the sky. He wanted darkness, but the night seemed to be taking its sweet time, content for now with the deep purple hue. In his eyes, this wasn't beauty and it wasn't God's glorious *mise en scène*. In his eyes, this was just another reminder that those who survived would still have to wake tomorrow.

In his pocket, his phone started to vibrate. The first and second calls he ignored, but on the third, he took it out and looked at the screen. After he finally accepted the call, Amanda said hello once, and she said it twice before he wound up and threw the device as far as he could. He didn't even watch it down. He wanted her to make that fall alone.

* * *

"You sure he's here?" Alice asked after Ashok put the car into park.

"Him, I am not sure. His phone, however, that I am positive. Steve Jobs has yet to lie to me."

"I don't see him anywhere, Ashok," Alice said as she scanned the area.

"That is why we should get out and walk around."

Ashok and Alice exited the vehicle. She interlaced her hand within his and led him to the security rail. For a moment, they both stared out. She had her head on his shoulder, and he had an arm around her waist.

"God, it's so powerful and majestic."

"Like the moon, it is leaving us. In fifty thousand years it will no longer be here."

"Why?" Alice questioned.

"The Niagara River is eating it. Every year it dines on about a foot. So, in fifty thousand years, it will pull back to Lake Erie and no longer exist."

"And the moon, when is it breaking up with us?"

"It is not the moon that is breaking up with us. It is us who are breaking up with it. We are pushing it away. We are transferring our energy to it, and so it is speeding up. And as we have learned, the faster an object is orbiting another object, it starts to move away."

"How long do we have left with our friend?"

"I believe it is about fifty billion years."

"That is so long. I wonder why we even think about it."

"Because we can, I suppose. But it won't matter though. In one billion years the sun will begin to expand, and as it does so, it will start to melt the earth."

"It is so sad that everything ends, isn't it?"

"Yes, it is quite sad if you believe it that way. That is why you should think of becoming a Hindu. At least with us, all of this is only a cycle. People are reincarnated and so is the universe. After this big bang is over, then there is another one and so on and so on."

On the cheek, Alice gave Ashok a kiss. And as she was doing so, she spotted Evan a good fifty feet down the way. He was on the wrong side of the security rail. He was steps from the edge. She let Ashok know that she had located him and they hurried over to where he was standing.

"Brother, you should not be on that side," Ashok called out. When his friend didn't acknowledge him, he spoke again. "Brother, do you hear me?"

"My cell phone, huh?" Evan finally replied.

"Yes, that is correct. I followed the signal all the way from the airport."

"Well, we don't need to worry about that anymore," Evan said, though he spoke it so softly that none of the words were able to rise over the sound of the raging waters below.

"You should come on this side. Someone is going to think you are getting ready to jump."

"If they thought that, Ashok, they would be in the wrong tense. I've already jumped a thousand times."

"I am not following you," Ashok replied after glancing at Alice with a look of alarm.

"My soul, Ashok. Since I've been here, I've thrown it over a thousand times. What you see now is all that remains."

"I am sorry to hear that. Is it the girl Amanda?"

"No, it was the girl Emily. Today she died. She was only eight. Can you imagine that, Ashok, only eight? How does a little girl just die? That was not fair to her."

"You are right, my brother. That was not fair to her. It is too young to live and then to die. There should not be deaths like that. They have no meaning."

"Evan, why don't you come on this side, okay?" Alice said, now starting to worry a little more than she had been. When he didn't return with an answer, she turned to Ashok and said in a whisper, "Go get him."

With a foot on the lower rail and his hands on the top bar, Ashok pushed himself up and hopped over. A few steps taken, and now he was beside his friend. He reached an arm around Evan's body to lay a hand of empathy on his shoulder. He then squeezed tight to secure any passionate thoughts his friend may have been entertaining.

"I don't want to be me any longer, Ashok. I really don't. I wish it was possible that every time I looked in the mirror from here forward, there would be no reflection at all. I never want to see myself again."

"I understand this."

"I loved her, Ashok. I loved her like God. I loved her with all of my heart. But you know what I found out today?"

"What is that?"

"That our hearts are not made for that kind of love. They are not that strong. Our hearts they tear so easily. They are only made to love a little. We are little."

"You have become wise, my brother," Ashok replied to that.

"With wisdom comes the death of everything else, isn't that right?" Evan asked, and for the first time in the conversation, turned to Ashok for an answer.

"Come, let's get you back to where you are staying."

Ashok ushered Evan back to the security rail. Alice helped him over. She then collected him into her arms. He was lifeless, a mannequin. A look of assistance she threw to Ashok. One nod of a head was returned to let her know to keep holding him until he was able to breathe for himself again.

DO NOT
RESUSCITATE

THE CLOCK WENT FROM THREE thirty-one to three thirty-two. It went from five forty-five to five forty-six. No matter how he tried, he couldn't seem to find a place to hide yesterday from his mind. At exactly ten after eight, the sun snuck through the curtains of the motel room and rudely introduced itself. He wanted nothing to do with the unwanted guest and so got out of the chair he had been sitting in. Near the air conditioner, he picked up his backpack from the floor. The chain and lock undone, he had the door open an inch when he looked over to the bed. Alice and Ashok were entwined like vines, and he wished that he could have been either of them. He wished he could have been anyone but the skin that he was in.

Alice awoke just as the door closed and the lock reengaged. She eased herself out of bed so as not to disturb Ashok. The new light blinded her momentarily, and so she raised a hand to her face until her eyes could adjust to the strain. Evan was standing just outside the motel, his back to her and the stuffed bunny fastened to his backpack.

"You found a flight out, huh?" Alice said after walking over to where he stood.

"No, I'm going to take Amtrak back home. I need some time to just stare out a window and think," Evan replied, his eyes wandering from object to object across the street and his mind fixed on all the emptiness that in front of him now lay.

"Did you already call for a car?"

"Lost my phone at the Falls."

"I'll go wake, Ashok. We can drive you," Alice said and made a start for the motel room. Evan immediately called her back.

"No, let him sleep. It's not that far from here. I'll call him when I get back to Chicago."

"I wish there was some way I could mend your heart, Evan."

"Yeah, me too," he answered, and then exhaled a long breath to keep the tears from arriving again. "God, this life can just suck."

"It can. And I wish I could tell you it gets better. But all those things we ever love, they just end up being visitors. Once you realize that, then you don't have to be sad and you don't have to be afraid."

"All the good advice, it always arrives too late."

"I know."

"So," Evan said after a check of his watch told him it was time to start getting on his way, "are you guys staying?"

"I think we're going to hang out here for a few more days and have a look around. Any suggestions?"

"No, nothing I can think of."

"Okay," Alice said and then kissed him on the cheek. "We love you, Evan. You know that, right?"

He nodded. He gave her a little bit of a smile. He took his first steps away from her, then stopped.

"Alice."

"Yeah?"

"Ashok's a great guy, isn't he?"

"Yeah, he is."

"I'm really glad the two of you met."

"Me too. It's funny, it's like we were destined to meet."

"Some destinies are better than others, aren't they?"

"Yeah, some are better."

* * *

Evan had just crossed the motel parking lot when he heard the release from the air brakes of the city bus. He looked over. The bus continued on its way, but there he could see that the passenger it had dropped off was Amanda. He gave her only a momentary look and continued on his way. She took the straightest path to intercept him, and within a minute or so, was now walking a few feet behind. She still had on what she wore when they rushed her to the hospital. She had on faded blue jeans, and she had on combat boots. She had on a lifeguard's white and red T-shirt. Above the cross, she had asked for the words "DO NOT" to be placed. Below it, she had requested the print shop to put: "RESUSCITATE."

"I figured you'd be leaving. That's a good move." Evan

ignored her and kept moving forward. "Yeah, I wouldn't talk to me either. Anyway, I um . . . I just wanted to say I'm sorry about everything. I didn't want it to come to this. Not with you. Fuck, not with you, Evan."

Evan checked left and then checked right before crossing the street. Amanda followed without a look for herself. The metallic silver SUV slammed on its brakes to keep from hitting her. Evan glanced over his shoulder at the sound of the horn. Amanda didn't care and didn't even bother to see how close the fender had come to her knees.

"You know, I wanted to say it back to you when you told me you loved me. I don't know why the fuck I didn't. Maybe it would have changed everything if I did, huh? Yeah, maybe there's some other parallel world where the last few days never happened and we're still together."

Evan and Amanda crossed under a viaduct. From where they were, the Amtrak station was now only a few hundred yards or so away. He was wishing it was closer. He was wishing he was already on the train and she was even less than a faint memory. She was hoping he would just stop. She was hoping he had at least something to say. For him, those last steps seemed to take an eternity to reach. For her, it was maybe a few seconds before she was watching him opening the door to head inside.

"Fuck. Stop. Will you. Jesus Christ."

He closed his eyes for a moment. It was long enough for the door to fall against his shoulder, and it was long enough for her to get in a few more words.

"Just so you know, I'm hurting more than you. Christ, I've lost

John and Tommy in the same week. I can barely breathe right now if that makes you happy."

"You're not hurting more than me," he rebutted faster than she expected and in a tone that made her sense the hate.

The door was all she was looking at now as he had gone inside. Her head she lowered to have a vacant look at the ground. She was wondering just what the fuck he could have been talking about. A few moments passed, and the decision was made to follow him in. He was nowhere inside, though. He had already exited the small Amtrak station and was now standing on the platform waiting for his train.

Amanda walked up to Evan. He kept his back to her, and so with both hands, she gave him a shove. When he didn't turn around, she pushed him again, and this time he finally rotated to face her.

"How the fuck could you say you're hurting more than me? People died whom I knew and loved. You, on the other hand, just got let down by someone of inconsequence."

"That's not it."

"If it isn't that, then what the fuck is it?"

"Forget it."

"No, I'm not going to forget it. I swear, I'll get on the goddamn train with you and ride it all the way back to Chicago if I have to."

"Christ, Amanda. Stop talking. Just stop talking. I'm hurting because in between all of your deaths, I lost someone, too."

"Who? Who in the hell did you lose?"

"The little girl who lived next to you. Emily. She died yesterday."

"Emily? There's no one next to me named Emily. What the fuck are you talking about?"

"That really doesn't surprise me at all that you don't even know who she is. You've gone through this world in such a heroin cloud that all the precious things around you got lost in the daze, didn't they?"

"What happened to her?"

"I'm not talking about it."

"Tell me, Evan."

"You don't need to know."

"Goddammit, Evan. Tell me."

"Okay, maybe you do need to know. Maybe you need to understand that all of your actions aren't just self-inflicted wounds. That they have consequences you've been too blind to see."

"Are you going to fucking tell me or not?"

"The first night outside your apartment I ran into her and her father after you went in. He was taking her to the hospital. The next morning I went to visit her, and we became friends. Yesterday when I found you, I was supposed to be at the hospital before she went in for surgery. A surgery to ease the pressure from an incurable brain tumor. And I promised her I would be there. But I never made it because I was caught up in all of your drama. She died on the table, Amanda. I let down an eight-year-old girl because you had to shoot up once again. You know, there's only one thing I really need to understand."

"Yeah, and just what the hell is that?"

"Why you, Amanda? Why you? That's all I want to know.

Why does God keep giving you so many chances while everyone else around you dies?"

The words were a gunshot to her chest, and she started to breathe heavily as if her lungs had suddenly collapsed. Slowly, she started to backpedal away from everything. The rectangular sign mounted to the brick wall of the Amtrak station began flashing "EXPRESS" in digital red. She caught it from the corners of her eyes, and then she saw that from around the bend, a train was racing toward them. She looked to her right, she looked to the rails below. There she saw a rabbit sitting on a wooden railroad tie in the middle of the tracks. There she saw it twitching its nose at a patch of grass pushed up through the crushed stones. To the edge of the platform she walked over and slowly turned around. She gave him a smile that was serious and grave. She gave him a quick wave that was half-mast at her waist.

"Amanda!" Evan yelled as he watched her hop down. "Amanda!" he shouted again as he ran toward her.

The train sounded its horn and Evan gave a glance to see how much time she had left.

"I didn't mean it. I'm sorry. Get back up here. Please get back up here."

She was on one knee now. She was facing the rabbit and she was facing the train. The pleas from above seemed like muffled screams from an underwater dream. Her hand she held out, and just as she had intended, the rabbit scampered off. She then stood up and then she closed her eyes. Her body she stiffened. All the thoughts in her mind she set free. The train then granted her wish. The train it took her from life to death.

Evan gave in to gravity. His knees bent first and then his body followed. In his head, the words from his cousin kept playing on repeat: *All those things we ever love, they just end up being visitors. Once you realize that, then you don't have to be sad and you don't have to be afraid.* It was of no solace, though. What pain Amanda had finally unchained for herself, he understood was now his to live and breathe. *One death and the living all fall,* he thought.

Virginia Austin

Acknowledgments

Kimmy, my love, and Keira, my sweet, sweet little girl.

To my sisters, Holly and Chrissy, you are both dear treasures to me. And my only regret is that I didn't look for you sooner.

Rita Chiovari for her editing. Ken and Patrice Hugo. Brooke, Travis, Cody, Adam, and Jake Hugo. Cheryl and Frank Trikur. The Komada Family. Dave Hochfelder, Joe Laverdure, Aldo Liberio, Dave Ojeda, Jim Zab. Kathryn Gadomski and Chris Medack, Brad Gadomski and Emily Dutson.

Please think about the following organizations or others that are similar:

The ALS Association Greater Chicago Chapter; 220 W Huron, Suite 4003; Chicago, IL 60654; 312-953-0000

Haymarket Center; 932 W. Washington; Chicago, IL 60607; 312-226-4357

To my mother and father, Helen Virginia Brezinski and William Austin Duffy, although you are no longer with me, a day does not pass that I do not hear you whispering into my mind.